S0-AIL-125

"Mr. Cassidy, I'm in Trouble, Bad Trouble."

Butch Cassidy's keen eyes evaluated him, and a slight frown stamped his face at what he saw. This kid sure looked like he was in trouble. His face was pasty, and Cassidy could almost swear that Kale's voice was near the breaking point.

"You better come in and tell me all about it," he said matter-of-factly.

Cassidy sat down on the edge of the bed and waved Kale to a chair. "What's got you in such a sweat? It had to happen fast. You sure didn't look like this when you left here."

Kale locked his hands together to keep them from shaking. He kept his eyes on them. He had to have something to focus his attention on. Oh God. He was afraid he was going to break down.

Kale's first attempt to speak came out as a rasping croak. He swallowed hard and said in a jerky voice, "I just killed my brother."

LURE OF THE OUTLAW TRAIL

GILES A. LUTZ

BALLANTINE BOOKS • NEW YORK

*All of the characters in this book are fictitious, and any re-
sembulance to actual persons, living or dead, except for
historical personages, is purely coincidental.*

Copyright © 1979 by Giles A. Lutz

All rights reserved. Published in the United States by Ballantine
Books, a division of Random House, Inc., New York, and
simultaneously in Canada by Random House of Canada, Limited,
Toronto, Canada.

Library of Congress Catalog Card Number: 78-19333

ISBN 0-345-28599-9

This edition published by arrangement with Doubleday &
Company, Inc.

Manufactured in the United State of America

First Ballantine Books Edition: January 1980

LURE OF THE
OUTLAW TRAIL

Chapter One

Spring was always late coming to the high country. The stretch of the Continental Divide in the southwestern corner of Wyoming was about as tough a land as a man could choose to live in. The winters were long and cold, clamping down on everybody's spirits. Those drab, gray days eroded a man's tolerance of others, until he was as touchy as a wounded bear. Lifelong friendships had shattered under the savage onslaught of those brutal winters. Husband and wife often reached the last few days of the winter barely speaking to each other. Even whole families reached such a quarrelsome stage that, even if no actual violence broke out, the relationships became strained and as brittle as a fresh skim of ice.

Men looked eagerly toward spring. Spring was the season of mending and restoring the spirit. The suspicious, mean cussedness vanished with the melting of the snow pack.

Verl Wakeman rode into the corral and swung down. He was a long, lanky man, moving with the agility of a squirrel traveling through the treetops. His face was grave in repose, almost foreboding, but an infectious gleam of humor lurked in his gray eyes. He was twenty-five years old, and as strong as an oak. His hands were as big and hard as an oak burl. He pushed his hat to the back of his head, and his unruly reddish-blond hair fell down across his eyes. He set about stripping off the harness and bridle from his horse.

He slapped the bay gelding on its rump, and the affectionate slap sent the gelding scampering across the corral. The horse wasn't frightened, for he knew his

1

owner too well, just as Verl knew the horse. Neither would willingly do harm to the other.

"Look at him," Verl said and chuckled. "Full of vinegar. He knows spring is coming."

Owen Wakeman finished stripping the gear from his chestnut and grumbled, "I'm sure glad something knows." Only in years was he different from his brother. He was four years younger and cast in the same mold. The family resemblance was very strong between them. It showed in the lean, carved faces, in the way their level, gray eyes appraised a situation.

"Hell, Owen," Verl retorted. "You know it too. You were the one who pointed out the new buds on the aspen trees. You saw how the snow's melted on the high pasture. In spots, the grass was enough to carry stock."

"You make me sick," Owen said crossly. At Verl's raising eyebrows he said, "You're always looking at the bright side of things. Don't you ever come down to earth?"

Verl grinned at the upbraiding. That wasn't like Owen. He knew what was wrong with his brother, though he wisely didn't comment. The winter had been unusually severe, making trips to South Pass City difficult and, for long stretches of time, impossible. It had been too long since Owen had seen Etta Faber.

Verl's grin kept broadening. "Every day you sound more like the twins."

Kale and Kyle Wakeman were the two younger brothers, only eighteen years old. They were unhappy and sullen, always looking at the bleak side of everything.

"Don't you accuse me of that," Owen said sourly. "By God, if I thought I was turning out like them, I'd shoot myself."

Verl laughed and threw an arm affectionately across Owen's shoulders. "I wouldn't blame you," he said and chuckled. The twins were a constant bane on the lives of the Wakemans. How many times had Verl wanted to cuff some manners into them? Only a couple of hundred, he thought dourly. If it wasn't for Jabez's stern eye and heavy hand, it would have happened. He wouldn't have to administer that beating often, Verl

2

thought. One or two thorough thrashings would bring about a drastic change in the twins' attitude.

"Where in the hell were they?" Owen burst out. "Weren't they supposed to ride with us this afternoon?" His eyes suddenly narrowed. "Say," he howled. "Do you suppose they went into South Pass?" His face was too flushed, his breathing too rapid.

Verl knew what was happening to Owen. Every time Owen heard of the twins going into South Pass City, it drove him wild.

"Cut out that kind of thinking," Verl said brusquely. "You're going to drive yourself crazy."

The flush didn't lessen in Owen's face, and his breathing had a queer rasp.

"Come on, Owen," Verl begged. "Use your head. Say they *did* go into South Pass. That doesn't mean that Kale will try to go near Etta."

"Yes, he will," Owen said grimly. "He tries to see her every time he sneaks off to town. I told him the next time I caught him around her, I'd beat his head off."

Verl sighed. He guessed there was nothing more consuming than youthful jealousy. The sad part was that Owen was probably right. Kale was showing too much interest in Etta. That interest had grown once he learned how Owen felt about her. Out of pure devilment, Kale would torment Owen just for the pleasure of seeing him steam. This whole thing fit Kale's and Kyle's character well. Once they saw how much someone else cared for something, they wanted the same thing. Someday that avid greed was going to get their heads blown off.

"Simmer down, Owen. You're letting your imagination run away with you."

"Maybe," Owen growled. "But I've caught him looking at her calf-eyed several times. I've tried to tell him he isn't welcome at Etta's, but did you ever know either of them to take advice?"

Verl had to agree with that. There was a wide, perverse streak in the twins that delighted in hurting people. Owen's warning to stay away from Etta would be enough to make Kale deliberately seek her out.

There was one angle to this that worried Verl. Ow-

3

en's warning would be ineffectual. The warning should come from Etta. If she said, flatly, she didn't want to see Kale Wakeman again, it would be as effective as a slammed door. But would she? Verl didn't know. Etta Faber was a bright-eyed sprite of a girl. Her restless spirit sought out controversy. The more men who were interested in her, the more delighted she was. Verl didn't dare voice his judgment to Owen. To Owen she was the most wonderful thing ever created. Jealousy was hot-blooded; it was also blind.

Verl sighed as he envisioned ominous storm clouds ahead.

"You're fretting unnecessarily," Verl said in a consoling tone. "All Etta has to do is look at you, then compare what she sees in Kale. She's not a dumb girl. That should show her what she's got."

Owen wasn't completely pacified. "It'd better," he growled. "I'm telling you, Verl, if I ever catch him hanging around her house again, I'll break his damned neck."

They could stand out here jawing until night fell, and it wouldn't solve a thing. "Let's go in the house, Owen. Maybe Jabez knows where the twins went. He might have sent them off on some errand. Won't you feel stupid if you find out how useless all this stewing was?"

"Maybe," Owen conceded. The stubborn set didn't leave his face. "But I'm telling you—"

"I know," Verl interrupted. "You told me before. You couldn't have said it any plainer."

He punched Owen on the biceps and said, "Let's go get some hot coffee. Spring may be here, but the wind's still got a bite to it. I'm chilled to the bone."

They fell into step and walked out of the corral and headed toward the house. Verl looked at the small weather-worn house and shook his head. "It gets a little more beaten up with each passing year," he said mournfully. The house needed painting, and Verl winced at the repairs the house needed. Two things prevented them from getting at those repairs: lack of money and time. The momentary gloom faded, and he said half-humorously, "We're sure not getting rich."

"I could have told you that several years ago," Owen

4

said flatly. "I wonder why a man tears his guts out and winds up with barely enough money to live on."

Verl shook his head in rebuff. "Three things. Because he likes the country, he likes what he's doing, and there's always hope."

"Can't get very fat off of them," Owen observed.

They grinned at each other in a meeting of mind and spirit. "Never been a fat Wakeman in the family," Verl commented. "Be a shame to start now, wouldn't it?"

"No danger of that," Owen said and held the door open for Verl to enter.

They stepped into the small kitchen. Like the rest of the house, the room was cramped, particularly when all the Wakemans were gathered here. Jabez was busy stirring something on the stove. He looked over his shoulder. "What were you two arguing about? Heard you from clear outside."

"Not arguing," Verl said firmly. "Just agreeing on something."

Jabez turned from the stove and limped over to a chair and sat down. He was a barrel-chested man with a lined face. Age was responsible for some of that lining, but living with constant pain bore the greatest share. He was in his mid-fifties, and one could look at him, then at Owen and Verl, then say, "They're his boys, all right." He didn't have their healthy look, for he was gray. He grunted as he eased his right leg into a more comfortable position. A fall from a horse three years ago had changed Jabez's way of living. The doctor had done the best he could in repairing the shattered leg, but he shook his head as he said, "Bad break, Jabez. It'll cost you a lot of pain."

That doctor was too damned right. The ache in the leg was constantly with Jabez, particularly in a severe stress of weather. Winter gave him pure hell, and excessive moisture was bad too.

"Leg hurt, Pa?" Verl asked sympathetically.

"No more than usual," Jabez returned. He no longer could ride, and that galled him, for he loved the outdoors. Walking was out too, except for hobbling about the house. His life was confined to taking care of the house, preparing the meals, and keeping the books in order.

"What were you two talking about?" Jabez asked. He didn't like even the thought of disagreement between his two older sons. Rarely was the bond between them affected by a clash of opinion. He liked it that way. Thank God, there was harmony between these two.

"We were just discussing how fast we're getting rich."

Jabez grinned. "You don't think we're hitting a fast enough pace? We're not doing so bad. We own the land, and we're not too deep into the bank. I'm telling you, if the coming year is twice as good as the last two, we'll only lose about a third of what it costs us to raise a cow."

"That's good news," Owen said sardonically. He walked to the stove where coffee in the blackened pot was bubbling. He could expect that. Jabez was a genius at anticipating what was needed. Owen poured three cups and made two trips to set them on the table. He spooned sugar into his own cup. Jabez and Verl had learned to drink their coffee black.

"Not very encouraging, is it?" he commented. "If the weather doesn't whip us, the market does. Looks like we're playing with loaded dice."

Jabez's keen eyes studied Owen. "You're in a bad mood today, ain't you? We've gone through bad times before. We'll get through this one. Do you know of a better way of making a living?"

Owen stared at his cup. "A lot of people seem to. They get by with a hell of a lot less work and far better returns. South Pass City is filled with them."

"Ah," Jabez said softly. "You're talking about the outlaws. Why shouldn't South Pass be filled with them? It's on the outlaw trail."

Verl anxiously watched his father and brother. The outlaw trail was well-known throughout the West. It stretched from Montana to Mexico, passing through the roughest country imaginable. Rough country bred rough men. Some of the most infamous names in western history had sought shelter along that trail. A few lawmen had tried to dig out a wanted man from the rugged canyons and escarpments. Only a few had suc-

6

ceeded. Two things were against them: the country, and the lack of knowledge of the terrain. If a man didn't know where the few water holes and springs were located, he would perish miserably. It was easy to understand why the majority of the lawmen shrugged and let a wanted outlaw go. The outlaws knew the location of the sources of water.

"You thinking of joining the wild ones?" Jabez asked sharply. "Your ma and I had it tough too when we came out here." A momentary sadness dimmed his eyes. It always did at any mention of Laura Wakeman. She had died birthing the twins. Knowing the twins, Verl would say the exchange was a poor one.

"He's just talking to hear his brains rattle," Verl said, stepping in between a possible argument.

"By God, I hope so. Owen, how many outlaws do you know of who wound up old and comfortable? That easy money, as you call it, seems to dribble from their fingers. They usually wind up dead from a bullet or a rope. Is that what you want to look forward to?"

Owen gave Jabez an abashed grin. "You know better than that, Pa. Verl was right when he said I was talking to hear my brains rattle. But sometimes it does get wearing when things don't go smoother."

That appeased Jabez, for he chuckled. "Develops character, son. You may not wind up rich, but I can almost guarantee you one thing. Your chances at winding up old are reasonably good."

"Sure," Owen returned in a more amiable tone. "I guess this damned winter just about wore me out."

"Wore all of us out," Jabez said. "What did the high pasture look like?"

"Most of the snow is gone," Verl answered. "What hasn't melted, the wind's broomed away. We saw quite a bit of grass."

"Enough to carry stock now?" Jabez demanded.

Verl thoughtfully considered that. "I'd say so, Pa. How about it, Owen?"

Owen nodded. "It'll beat hell out of what the cattle have down here. Some spots may cause trouble, driving them up there, but it can be done. We bucked a few drifts, but we got through."

7

That reminded him of something, and he frowned.

Verl guessed at the reason for the frown, and he started to shake his head warningly at Owen. Jabez had enough burdens on his back without Owen dumping his personal troubles on him.

But Verl's attempt at a warning was too late, for Owen's words came tumbling out. "Where in the hell were Kyle and Kale this afternoon?" he demanded. "I thought they were supposed to ride with us."

Jabez's eyes sharpened as he caught the belligerence in Owen's face, but he said easily enough, "I found we were running short on supplies. I sent the twins into town in the buckboard to bring back what we needed. Hell, they wouldn't have done you much good anyway. They're daydreaming so much they rarely see what's right before their noses."

Owen savagely shook his head, and Jabez's eyes widened in surprise. "What's *that* supposed to mean?"

"Goddamn it, I don't want them going into South Pass," Owen yelled. "At least, not Kale. From now on, Verl or me will run whatever errands you need done."

Jabez was irked. It showed in the wave of color that stole through his cheeks. "That's hardly practical," he objected. "Neither Kale nor Kyle do much around here. They should do a little to earn their meals."

"Not going into South Pass," Owen said stubbornly.

Jabez leaned forward, his face intent. "You better tell me what this is all about." The quietness in his voice was ominous.

Owen went a beet-red, glanced helplessly at Verl, and saw no help there. Verl's stoic face said: You dug this hole; now you fill it up.

Owen sighed. "Maybe I'd better tell you all about it."

"That might be the wisest thing," Jabez said coldly.

"Kale's been hanging around Etta," Owen said. He wouldn't look at Jabez. He gulped several times before he could continue. "I told Kale to stay away from her, but you know how damned hardheaded he is."

Jabez nodded. "I know that."

Owen dared to glance at him. Perhaps his father did understand. If Jabez came down hard on Kale, it might make him stay clear of Etta.

8

"It seems to me that Etta has got the whole say-so here," Jabez went on. "If she doesn't want Kale hanging around, all she has to do is to say so."

Owen looked at the wall. His Adam's apple ran up and down his throat.

"Ah," Jabez said in reflection. "But she hasn't said so yet. Is that right?"

Owen nodded miserably.

"Looks like you're fencing pasture that don't rightly belong to you, Owen," Jabez said softly. "You better find out how she feels before you go about making a lot of hot talk."

"I know how she feels," Owen said obdurately.

"But Kale could be interested in her," Jabez pointed out. "It appears to me you're doing a heap of talking for people who really haven't authorized you to."

Owen squirmed under his father's scrutiny. "I don't think Kale is really interested in her. He's just keeping up his attentions to devil me."

"Could be," Jabez conceded. "You get some definite boundary lines established before you begin throwing your weight around. Then you can tell Kale what he can or cannot do."

Owen's face was stiff with resistance. "I'm not waiting any longer. I'm telling him the next time I see him he'd better stay away from her."

Jabez raised his shoulders, then let them fall. "You probably will," he admitted. "That stubborn streak runs a yard wide in every Wakeman I ever knew."

The silence fell heavy and oppressive. Each man at the table was occupied with his own thoughts. None of those thoughts were happy, Verl thought. He could say only one thing for certain. There was going to be the damnedest explosion and soon.

Chapter Two

The enticing aroma from a pot on the stove grew stronger, and Verl sniffed hungrily. "What's cooking, Pa?"

"Just stew, Verl. About all I had left until Kale and Kyle return." He glanced impatiently at the clock on the wall. "They should be back by now. They've been gone long enough."

Those words were enough to turn Owen's face black. He knew why the twins were gone for so long. He sat there, muttering to himself.

Verl shook his head. They'd never get through this evening without a quarrel at least. He just hoped it could be held down to that.

He sat there, thinking about Etta Faber and her sister Ann. The two sisters were as different as night and day. Verl knew from personal experience, for he visited Ann whenever he could. Ann was shy almost to the point of retiring. She didn't have Etta's flashy appearance, but Verl preferred Ann's beauty. Her beauty was the kind that would age gently, and although he had never voiced it, he intended to see that beauty age. Etta talked incessantly. Once she got an opening in a conversation, she never released it. Verl often wondered how Owen stood that constant chatter. But Owen worshiped Etta, and Verl gave him that right. Ann rarely ventured an opinion, and usually only after it was asked for. She had a keen and facile mind, and her eyes talked more eloquently than her tongue.

Verl mused on the differences that ran in families. He knew all about those differences, for he had seen them develop in his own family. It was hard to believe that with the same parents, offspring could be so entirely different. Look at him and Owen and the twins. Ann and Etta were another example. He half smiled as he thought of Etta and Ann, wondering if they often crossed swords. In privacy, he would bet they did. The quiet kind like Ann could be pushed so far before they bowed their necks.

Jabez got up, limped to the stove, and stirred the stew. "Ain't gonna wait much longer for them to come back. I'll have to take the stew off the fire, or let it burn up."

He looked at Verl. "What are you grinning about?"

Verl wasn't aware he was grinning. "Didn't know I was. I was just thinking about how family members can be so different. Same blood, the same raising. You'd think kids would turn out at least somewhat alike. But it doesn't work that way."

Jabez sat down. "It sure as hell doesn't." He didn't mention Kyle and Kale, but Verl knew what Jabez meant. "Beats hell out of me, Verl. Look at you and Owen, and you know immediately you came out of Laura and me. But the twins—" He shook his head. "If I didn't know Laura was a faithful wife, I'd swear those two came out of a different pod." He grimaced. "Sometimes I can't help but wonder at some of the things those two do."

"You don't have to prove anything to me," Owen said crossly. "Many a time I haven't been able to believe those two are my brothers."

Jabez levelly observed him. "Well, they are, and don't you forget it."

"I wish to hell I could," Owen said gloomily.

Jabez started to say something, then turned his head toward the door. "Thought I heard the rattle of wheels. Maybe that's them. For God's sake, don't stir up any trouble tonight. Let's eat one meal in peace."

Verl nodded, though he knew the words weren't directed at him.

"I'll try," Owen said flatly. "But sometimes their damned cockiness rakes me raw."

Verl wanted to say, You're not alone, but he held the words. That would give Owen encouragement to say

11

something more, and Verl knew how badly Jabez wanted peace.

He turned in his chair as the door opened. Kale came in first, his arms laden with packages. Kyle was right on his heels, and his arms, too, were burdened.

At first glance, one would say they were identical twins, but the Wakeman family knew better. Kale was a fraction of an inch taller, but both of them were short, swarthy men. They had black eyes where Verl's and Owen's were gray. A scowl usually rode their faces, for rarely were they happy. About the only thing that could draw laughter was someone else's discomfort. A hard fall would evoke gales of laughter. They were in the Wakeman family, but from all appearances, they didn't really belong.

"You gonna give us a hand unloading?" Kyle asked in a sulky tone. "Pa ordered enough stuff to damned near empty the store."

Verl started to rise, but Owen checked him. His face was frozen. Just thinking about Kale seeing Etta made him seethe inwardly.

"Is there any job you two can do without begging help?" Owen drawled.

Verl expected Jabez to come down hard on Owen, but Jabez merely looked pained. Already his request for a peaceful evening was on the verge of being shattered.

Kyle's dark countenance turned even darker. "What's eating on you?" he snapped. "We don't need your damned help. You can go to hell as far as I'm concerned."

Owen grabbed the edge of the table and started to rise.

"Hold it," Verl said quietly. "You're forgetting what Pa asked you."

That slowed Owen, for he let go of the table and settled back into his chair. But the stubborn jut remained in his jaw.

Verl could safely bet this evening wouldn't pass without a more serious outbreak.

He got to his feet and said easily, "I'll give you a hand."

Kale and Kyle glared at him. They were easily offended and slow to forgive a real or imaginary offense. "We don't need any help from any of you."

They slammed down their packages on the counter, spun on their heels, and whipped out of the door.

Jabez stared straight ahead, his jaw set hard.

Verl tried to break the tension. "Well, they're keeping their record intact. Always pleasant to be around."

Owen winced. "My fault, Pa. I guess I really wanted to provoke them."

Jabez sighed deeply. "It doesn't matter, Owen. If it wasn't one thing, they'd find another." His attempt at a smile was a failure. "Kinda tough living around them, isn't it?"

"This'll pass," Verl said quietly. Just as the countless other squabbles had simply worn out. He kept hoping while the twins were growing up that their dispositions would change, and they would mature. His hopes were futile. Kale and Kyle grew more unruly with the passing years.

"This could be my fault," Jabez said reflectively. He nodded solemnly at the startled glances Verl and Owen gave him. "It could be," he insisted in a low voice. "Do either of you remember when the twins were born?"

Owen shook his head, but Verl nodded. "I remember, Pa," he answered. "I think that was the last moment of peace this house has known," he said musingly.

Kale and Kyle were the noisiest babies he had ever been around. Nothing seemed to pacify them. Once they learned that crying was a sure way to get attention, they never stopped. Those two had run three housekeepers out, and all three had been aggressive, determined women. But they had given up against the indomitable will of the twins.

"After their ma died," Jabez went on, "Kale and Kyle were sickly babies. I felt guilty, as though somehow it was my fault. I gave them their way in everything, even after they grew out of babyhood." His eyes were far away, as though he looked at something distant. "I know now I should have walloped the hell out of them. Maybe that would have changed them."

"Naw," Owen said decisively. "You're too rough on

13

yourself, Pa. Every newborn colt looks the same, doesn't it?"

Jabez nodded slowly, but his eyes were puzzled. He didn't get what Owen was driving at.

"All colts get about the same treatment," Owen went on. "But some of them have a streak of cussedness in them that can't be knocked out. They grow up bad despite the efforts made to change them."

Jabez's mouth was a big O as he understood. "No," he disclaimed. "You're talking about animals, Owen. Not people. You can't judge the two the same way."

"I think it's the same," Owen insisted. "Nothing could have changed the twins."

Maybe Owen had something there, Verl thought. God knew Jabez had done everything a father could do, and he hadn't been able to erase that nasty streak in Kyle and Kale. "It could be, Pa," he said softly. He felt a rush of pity for his father. Jabez had carried a tremendous load on his shoulders all those years. If Jabez could accept the possibility of Owen's theory, it might lighten some of that burden of guilt. "You think about it, Pa," Verl said gently.

"I'll think about it," Jabez said dully. There was no promise in his voice. "Maybe I'm lucky, at that. You two sure didn't turn out like they did. Maybe a man can consider himself fortunate if fifty per cent of his offspring turn out well."

Verl stood and came around the table to lay an affectionate hand on Jabez's shoulder. "That's the way to look at it," he said heartily. "There's always the hope that something might happen to open Kale and Kyle's eyes."

Before Jabez could answer, the twins came back in with the remainder of their purchases.

They glanced furtively at their family, their eyes filled with suspicion. The look accused the three of talking about them.

"Is that all?" Verl asked. He was determined to remain pleasant despite how the twins reacted.

"Do you see us going back after more?" Kale snarled.

Verl felt his muscles tighten. God, how he'd like to

14

beat some common manners into these two. He caught the barely perceptible warning in Jabez's eyes and forced himself to relax.

Owen wasn't relaxing, for Verl heard the hoarse rasp of his breath.

"You boys get washed up," Jabez said. "Supper's just about ready."

"All right," Kale growled and led the way outdoors.

"A human tongue wasn't built to talk to those two," Owen said shakily. "A club would do a hell of a lot better job. I'm beginning to believe that's the only thing they'll ever understand."

"Drop it, Owen," Verl said firmly.

Owen darted a glance at Jabez, swallowed hard, then said a weak, "Sure."

Verl hoped Owen would stick to his word.

Chapter Three

Verl carried the pot around the table and ladled out the stew. He filled Kale's plate, then asked, "That enough, Kale?"

Kale's suspicious eyes darted at Verl. He didn't trust anything or anybody. He decided Verl wasn't trying to make a fool of him and growled, "Enough for now, I guess."

"Sure," Verl said and took the pot back to the stove. He sliced a fresh loaf of bread and said in an ordinary tone, "Good thing you two brought bread back with you. We were plumb out." He carried the coffeepot and the bread to the table. He poured coffee all around before he sat down. He or Owen tried to save Jabez all the steps they could.

For a few minutes, hunger eliminated the need of conversation. When the first sharp onslaught of hunger was eased, Verl asked, "Anything unusual happen in town this afternoon, Kale?"

Kale's black eyes were filled with suspicion. "What's that supposed to mean?" he asked in a surly tone.

Owen flashed Kale an angry glance, and his face was red again. He jumped to the conclusion that Kale's evasiveness was to cover his visit to Etta.

Verl swore at himself for asking that question. You could ask Kale something about the weather, and his answer would rile you. My God! It was impossible to get through a peaceful evening. They couldn't even make it through a harmonious meal.

"It doesn't mean anything," Verl replied. He kept his voice even, though it was difficult. "I thought you might have seen something interesting."

Verl groaned silently. Damned if he wasn't fumble-tongued tonight. He was saying everything wrong. He had no intention of making reference to Etta, but Owen would take it that way. Owen's face was flaming again.

Owen glared at Kale, his eyes shooting sparks.

Kale, don't say you stopped by to see Etta, Verl begged mentally. Owen's ready to go up right now. Just the wrong word, and he'll come across the table at you.

Kale looked at Owen's rage-congested face and grinned maliciously. Owen was burning, and Kale got great enjoyment out of that.

"If you meant, did I see Etta?" Kale paused, letting the moment drag out. "I didn't," he finally finished. "With all the shopping Pa wanted done, I didn't have time."

Verl was afraid his sigh of relief would be heard. He dared look at Owen. Some of the blackness was leaving his face, and his breathing was returning to normal.

"We found something more interesting," Kyle spoke up. "We ran into Butch Cassidy and Kid Curry." His face held almost a reverent awe.

"You should've run into more of the Wild Bunch," Jabez said sourly. "I heard they were wintering in South Pass."

"We only talked to Butch Cassidy and the Kid," Kyle said. "Damn but they treated us good. They wouldn't let us buy a single drink."

The silence grew oppressive. Verl could almost guess what Jabez was thinking. Jabez was an honest man, and he couldn't stand even the mention of the Wild Bunch. Verl knew Butch Cassidy and Kid Curry by sight only. Cassidy was a man of average height, weighing around a hundred and seventy pounds. His face was almost square, and he had the coldest, deepest blue eyes Verl had ever seen. There was a small red scar under his left eye. Cassidy was the mastermind of the Wild Bunch, and legend and reality attributed many a daring holdup to him. When a man had remained free as long as Cassidy, it became difficult to separate legend from fact. Verl guessed Cassidy was smart enough, for as yet he hadn't been apprehended. He did arouse a loyalty in his followers, for most of the Wild Bunch had been with him for several years. Cassidy had an unwritten agreement with the people of South Pass and the ranchers in the surrounding country. He didn't steal from them, and in turn, they left him alone. Verl suspected several of those people even aided Cassidy whenever they could. He had heard several ranchers speak favorably of him. Cassidy had been known to give a struggling rancher a hand with money or a few needed horses.

Kid Curry was an entirely different matter. He was called The Tramp, for the sloppy way he dressed; Tiger of the Wild Bunch; and a half-dozen more unsavory names. His real name was Harvey Logan, and he was mean clear through. He killed for the sheer pleasure of killing, where Cassidy was interested only in profit.

"Did you enjoy their company?" Jabez asked. His voice was ominously quiet.

"Hell, yes." Kale and Kyle spoke in unison. "There's a couple of smart men. They don't wear their asses out trying to make a living chasing a few cows around, and their pockets are filled with money."

It's coming, Verl thought, and a tightness stole through his body. Jabez had begged for a harmonious evening. Evidently, he had forgotten all about that.

"Their pockets are filled with stolen money," Jabez said passionately. "Those two never did an honest day's work in their life. I'll take that back. Cassidy did learn an honest occupation. He was a butcher. That's where

17

he gets that nickname. But butchering was too slow for him. He found out that stealing was a whole lot easier."

Kale and Kyle stared at their plates. Both laid down their forks, and Verl noticed how tightly their hands were clenched.

"I still say those two are smart," Kale said doggedly.

This impudence outraged Jabez, and he shouted, "I'll tell you just how smart they are. If they don't wind up dead, they'll spend a lot of their lives in prison. If they live to come out, they'll be broken, old men. Is that what you want?"

Jabez had said something on the same order to Owen. The difference was that Owen listened. Verl doubted that a single word Jabez said penetrated Kale's and Kyle's thick skulls.

Jabez saw the implacable set of their faces and gave up. "Have it your way," he said wearily. "Keep on thinking the way you're going, and neither of you will live to be very old."

Verl saw the wild flash of temper in the twins' eyes. It was time to break up this conversation before it became more heated.

"Did I tell you that I heard about Indian Charley a couple of weeks ago?" Verl asked. "Bigley was by and told me that Indian Charley dropped dead in Sanderson's General Store. The doctor claimed it was a heart attack. Poor old Charley." Verl shook his head. "He never did anybody any harm. He just minded his own business. I wonder how many miles he walked from his shack to town."

Indian Charley was another legend around South Pass. In reality, he was more than a legend; he was a fact. Charley made his monthly trips into town to buy needed supplies, and he always paid for them with a gold nugget. Those nuggets were irregularly sized, some small, some larger. Verl suspected Charley had been cheated often, for he never got any change from his nugget. But that never seemed to bother Charley. Perhaps he rested secure in the knowledge that there were more where that nugget came from.

The legend sprang up with the speculation as to where Charley got his money. Some claimed he had a rich hidden mine, and he only dug in it often enough to buy his monthly supplies.

Verl remembered Jabez and the family talking about Indian Charley. "I don't think he's got any great hidden wealth," Jabez said. "That ain't according to an Indian's nature. If he had that kind of wealth, he'd go on a spending spree that would knock your eyes out. No, I think he's found a small pocket and is smart enough to dole it out."

Verl and Owen had agreed with that opinion, but Kale and Kyle had voiced strenuous objection. "No," they had yelled. "He's got a big hidden mine. He's got enough Indian smart not to show it all at once. It's a rotten shame."

"What's a shame?" Jabez had asked.

"That a damned, stinking Indian has that kind of money."

Jabez's face was granite as he studied them. "Are you two thinking of doing something about that?"

"You're damned right we are," Kale said.

Verl remembered that conversation as vividly as though it happened only yesterday. The twins were only twelve, but they had diligently tried to track Charley to his hidden wealth. They had kept up the game until they were fifteen years old, then the lure had simply faded. Either they were convinced Charley had no mine, or his cleverness had worn them out.

Verl almost chuckled as he remembered how many nights the twins had come in completely tuckered out. *They* might not remember, or want to, but *he* did. He couldn't resist asking slyly, "You still believe in that mine?"

Kale's face flamed as he realized Verl was digging him. "We know it's still out there. That damned Indian just gave us the slip. One of these days, somebody's going to stumble across it, and he's going to be so rich it'll make everybody sick."

Verl disagreed with that, though he didn't say so. No, if Charley had a secret, it had died with him. The mine that the twins dreamed of wasn't going to be rediscovered. "Maybe," he said laconically and was willing to drop the subject.

Owen wasn't as charitable as Verl. The twins were embarrassed, and Owen enjoyed milking the moment. "That mine appeals to you, doesn't it?" he asked sarcastically. "You'd like to get rich overnight without having to work for it." He enjoyed the twins' discomfort, and he pressed on. "Listening to you talk about the Wild Bunch shows how your minds run. If you're smart, you'll listen to Pa and learn how to work for a living."

Kale sprang to his feet, his face contorted. "Goddamn it," he raved. "I don't have to listen to this crap of yours. I'll see anybody I want to and when I want to."

Owen leaned forward, his eyes savage. "What's that supposed to mean?" he asked sharply.

Kale had turned the tables, and the satisfaction was ugly on his face. "Just what I said. When I said I'll see anybody, that includes Etta. Anytime I want."

"You will like hell," Owen roared and jumped to his feet. "I've warned you before about slinking around her house. If you're wise, you'll stop it."

"You'll stop me?" Kale sneered.

"You can bet on that," Owen retorted. "If you want, I can start that lesson right now."

"Hold it, you two," Jabez roared. "Listening to you, no one would ever believe there's a drop of the same blood in you. I won't have any more of this."

Kale returned Jabez's furious gaze until he could no longer meet his father's eyes. *"He* started it," he mumbled. "I'm too old to have to listen to him."

"Maybe," Jabez conceded. "But you're not too old to listen to me."

Again Kale tried to meet his father's eyes and failed.

Kyle came to Kale's assistance by saying, "We don't have to stay here and listen to this."

Worry began ticking in Verl. That sounded as though they had made up their minds and might leave. He wouldn't be surprised if it turned out that way. When one of them made up his mind about something, the other usually followed suit.

"You're not going anyplace but to bed," Jabez said savagely. He studied both of them, then added, "Unless you're ready to make the break permanent. You leave, and you can't come back here when you find the going too hard."

Verl caught the indecision in the twins. Each waited for the other to make the break, but neither was mature enough to take such a final step. Verl would hate to see the family split up like this.

Kale made the first move. "Oh hell, Kyle. Let's go to bed." Jabez seemed to be holding his breath, and when he spoke his voice was normal and assured. "You're going to get up early in the morning. I want you two to drive some cattle up to the high pasture. Verl says it's ready."

Kale's face suffused with rage. "Why don't he and Owen drive 'em? They know the way better than we do. They've already been up there once."

"Because it's about time for you two to pitch in and do a little work around here," Jabez retorted. "You and Kyle are making that drive."

The show of authority put a whine in Kale's voice. "Kyle and me can't drive all those cattle up there by ourselves. We need help."

Jabez looked disgusted. "I'm moving forty head. That's all. If you two can't handle that many head, it's about time you turn in your spurs."

Kale muttered an oath as he followed Kyle out of the room.

Verl looked at Owen, then at his father. He whistled softly. "I thought they were going for sure this time." This had happened several times before, but when it came time to strike out on their own, the twins didn't have the gumption to face the unknown.

"So did I," Jabez confessed. "You know something, boys. I'd reached the point where I didn't give a damn if they did leave. If they picked this moment, I made up my mind I wasn't going to try and stop them."

Verl and Owen exchanged grins, and Owen said, "I say good. They've been too cocky for too long."

Jabez's eyes questioned Verl, and Verl nodded. "I feel about the same way, Pa."

"Then, that's settled." The relief was plain in Jabez's

21

tone. "I've made my move too late. I should have handled them different quite a few years back." He shook his head, and there was sorrow in the gesture. "I can tell you one thing for sure. It's coming, sure as hell."

Chapter Four

It was pure heaven, lying in bed with nothing stringent prodding him. Verl yawned and rolled over. Maybe he wouldn't get out of bed until noon. Owen was asleep, sawing away at a good rate. Verl listened in awed wonder. Owen's snoring always picked up more volume along toward morning. If Verl was asleep, he could go right through that snoring. But once he was awakened, he knew he would never reach that blissful oblivion again.

He lay there, listening for sound to come from the twins' room. He heard nothing, and he thought, Hell, they never get out of bed until they're kicked out. Then he remembered Jabez had set Kale and Kyle a task for today. They were supposed to drive cattle to the high pasture. Had they left already? It was possible, for Jabez had set an early hour for rising.

Verl grinned as he recalled the twins' indignation at being set a task. He might as well get up, he couldn't go back to sleep now. He stood and stepped into his jeans, then tugged on his boots. Should he awaken Owen? Naw, he thought, let him sleep.

A delicious aroma crept into the bedroom from the kitchen. Verl sniffed and knew what it was. Jabez was frying sourdough pancakes. Verl had better awaken Owen now. Owen would appreciate being called for breakfast more than getting a few additional winks of sleep.

Verl leaned over and shook Owen hard. You had to

22

be rough to drag Owen out of that deep cave he crawled into every night.

Owen knuckled his eyes and stared foggily at Verl. "You better have a good reason for waking me up," he said.

"Smell!"

Owen sniffed. "That's a good reason," he said solemnly. "Wait while I get dressed."

"Why should I?"

"So you won't beat me into the kitchen. As big a hog as you are for Pa's pancakes, once you get a start, Pa can't keep ahead of you."

Verl looked at his flat belly. "Sometimes I wonder myself where I put it all." He paused for a moment in the doorway. "Going to be a particularly pleasant breakfast. The twins are gone."

For a moment Owen's face was blank, then he grinned. "I remember now. They were supposed to drive those cattle. Did they really go?"

"Pa ordered them out early. As mad as he was when he went to bed, I don't think he'd let it pass. I didn't hear any stirring around in their room."

Owen whooped his elation. "This is one breakfast I'm really going to enjoy."

He finished dressing and joined Owen. They walked together into the kitchen.

Jabez had a hot fire going in the stove, and his face was flushed from the heat. "What was all that hollering about?" He lifted four pancakes out of the pan and deposited them on a plate.

"It was Owen," Verl replied. "He was tickled he didn't have to eat with the twins. I told him I thought they were gone."

Jabez nodded soberly. "They are. Slipped out of the kitchen just a few minutes ago." He grinned bleakly. "They didn't want anything to eat. All they took was coffee."

"They grouse at you, Pa?" Verl asked.

"Not a word. I guess my authority is still holding." He shook his head, and the gesture said he wondered how long that authority would hold.

"Sit down," Jabez said. "It's all ready."

23

He set a stack of cakes before Verl, limped back to the stove and returned with a second plate for Owen.

Verl poured the thick syrup on the cakes and watched it flow slowly over the edges. The aroma pleased his stomach, and he felt the juices flow into his mouth. Sourdough pancakes made about as good a breakfast as a man could want.

"How many can you eat?" Jabez asked.

"You know Verl," Owen said. "I'd say about fifty."

"You could be right," Jabez commented and turned back to the stove.

Verl cut into the cakes for his first bite and placed it into his mouth. His eyes closed in bliss. If there was a better pancake maker in the country, Verl hadn't found him.

He swallowed and reached his fork out for another bite. His hand froze. That ungodly squalling sounded as though it was right in the kitchen.

"What's that?" Owen cried.

Verl sprang to his feet. He knew what made that squall. "It's Jigger. One of the twins is trying to saddle him."

Owen's mouth sagged open. Jigger allowed only Verl to handle him. He raised undiluted hell whenever somebody else tried to take Verl's place.

"It couldn't be," he said weakly. "You've warned the twins about it often enough before."

Verl turned for the door. "Sounds like they forgot," he said grimly.

He headed for the door, not taking time to pick up his sheepskin. Owen was right behind him, and Jabez followed.

"I can handle this," Verl flung over his shoulder. He frowned. That wasn't stopping either of them.

The early-morning air bit at him, and he shivered. At this time of morning, spring seemed a hundred years away.

Verl was the first to reach the corral. He stepped inside, and neither Kale nor Kyle saw him. Kale had already saddled Jigger. It must have been quite a struggle, for his face was flushed.

"Stand still, damn you," Kale roared. He made an

24

attempt to put his boot into the stirrup, and Jigger danced away. Kale kicked at the gelding and missed.

Kyle held the reins, and he jerked on them to stop Jigger's crazy dancing. His broad grin showed how much he enjoyed this.

"I thought you were a horseman," he jeered.

"Just watch," Kale said grimly. "I'll knock some sense into that damned-fool horse's head. I'll quiet him down."

Verl's face was tight, the cheekbones standing out starkly. Kale meant what he said, for Verl had often seen him abuse animals. This was one time it wasn't going to happen.

He took a long, quick stride and reached out a hand just as Kale got a foot into the stirrup.

Kale started to swing up, and that furious hand clamped on his shoulder. Verl yanked Kale back with all of the force in his arm. The force propelled Kale along the ground, and he stumbled backward. He lost his balance and fell hard. His head rapped against the semifrozen ground, and he blinked dazedly.

Verl ran over and stood over Kale. Kale had seen him angry before, but nothing like this.

"Damn you," Verl raged. "I've told you before never to lay a hand on Jigger. What does it take to get something through your thick head?"

He was wild with fury, and it demanded release. He grabbed hold of Kale's coat lapels and jerked him to his feet.

"What do you think you're doing?" Kale squalled. The wildness in Verl's eyes made him uneasy. He licked his lips and went on, "My horse needed new shoes," he said weakly. "I didn't have time to replace them. I didn't think it'd hurt anything to borrow Jigger. I knew you weren't using him this morning."

If anything, the feeble explanation only increased Verl's anger. This was typical of Kale. He hadn't even bothered to ask Verl's permission to use Jigger.

"By God, it's about time you learned something," Verl said thickly.

He let the right fist go, wanting to smash that impudent face. The blow was a good one, but it went in a

25

little high, landing on Kale's cheekbone. At that, it had enough force to knock Kale over backward. He landed hard on his back.

He wasn't out. His movements were uncoordinated, and his face was slack. He tried to get his arms under him to lift himself off the ground.

He kept shaking his head as he muttered, "Goddamn you."

Kyle dropped Jigger's reins and flew at Verl. "Nobody hits Kale," he screeched.

Jigger snorted and scrambled across the corral. He stood at the far wall, his forehoofs beating at the ground, his eyes rolling.

"You too?" Verl roared. "You're in the same class as Kale. You don't learn any easier."

He waited until Kyle almost reached him, then whipped in another blow. This blow was better. It landed flush on Kyle's chin, knocking him off his feet. He landed in a limp heap and didn't move.

Verl heard Kale scream with rage. He whirled, and Kale was fumbling for his gun. Verl was a good ten feet from Kale, and he knew he would never be able to cover that much distance before Kale drew.

Owen was only a stride from Kale. He jumped and landed with a boot swinging. Kale completed his draw, but before he could point the muzzle, Owen's boot thudded into his wrist. Kale howled, and the gun went spinning through the air.

"Settle down, or I'll kick your damned head off," Owen snapped.

Kale looked up into that intent face. His wrist was throbbing, and he kept rubbing it.

"Nobody hits Kyle," he snarled.

"Verl just did," Owen pointed out. "Kyle said nobody hits you. Looks like Verl made damned liars out of both of you."

"I'll fix him for this. You wait and see." Kale was very near tears.

"I ought to stomp you good," Owen said in complete disgust. "Both of you asked for what you got. You knew Verl didn't allow anybody to take Jigger. Maybe this time you'll be convinced he means it."

26

"I'm going to fix him," Kale repeated.

"Say that once more, and I'll kick the hell out of you," Owen threatened.

Jabez limped up behind Owen and looked down at Kale. "Owen's right. You took Jigger against Verl's wishes. You deserved far worse than he gave you."

Kale was so furious he was almost incoherent. "He'll be the sorriest man in the world. You'll see."

Verl shook his head. When Kale got in one of these rages, there was no use trying to reach him. "Why don't you just shut up?" he asked wearily.

Kale fixed rage-inflamed eyes on Verl. "You think I'm just talking. You just wait—"

Jabez cut him off short. "Stop it," he roared. For an instant, they looked at each other—Kale sullenly defiant, Jabez struggling with a deep-seated fury.

"That's enough," Jabez said, as though reaching a final decision. "I've had enough. Get Kyle on his feet, then pack your things and get off this place."

That got through to Kale, and he was stunned. "You don't mean that, Pa." Enough kid remained in him to make his voice shaky. "Why, we were going to drive those cattle for you."

Jabez slashed the air with the edge of his palm. "I don't need you to move them. Verl and Owen will take care of them. Get out."

Again two pairs of eyes locked, one of them mutely begging, the other implacable.

Kale recovered some of his bluster. "To hell with you too," he shouted. "You always did favor those two over Kyle and me."

Jabez shook his head, and Kale misread the gesture. Jabez was weakening.

Jabez straightened out that false impression in a hurry. "You just made me see things clear. I should have kicked you off years ago. Get out. I won't tell you again."

Kale started to beg again, for his lips trembled. Then they clamped in a tight, ugly line. His face set with a new determination, and he yelled, "Who in the hell needs you? Kyle and me are going, but you're going to be one sorry man."

"You open your mouth again, and I'll shut it permanently," Verl snapped. "You heard Jabez. Get going."

Kale stared at each of the three in turn, and the hatred in those black eyes bubbled and seethed. He got to his feet, and neither Verl nor Owen offered to give him a hand. Kale finally made it. He brushed a mixture of mud and snow off his clothes, then looked at the gun lying on the ground.

Owen correctly interpreted the glance. "Don't get any fool ideas," he said.

"It's *my* gun," Kale howled.

Owen nodded. "Sure. I'll leave it for you at Sanderson's store the next time I go into town. Right now you need a little cooling off."

Kale glared at him, then walked over to where Kyle lay.

Kyle was coming to, and Kale helped him to his feet. Kyle leaned on him for momentary support.

"We've been kicked off, Kyle," Kale said loudly. "They don't want us around any more."

Kyle stared first at Verl, then at Owen. The last look rested longest on Jabez. Kyle's jaw was bruised and swollen. He touched the bruise gingerly.

"I won't forget this," he promised. "Who in the hell wants to live around those three?"

He angrily threw off Kale's supporting arm. "Let's get off this damned place. If I never see it again, I won't have lost anything."

The pair left the corral, detouring around where their father and brothers stood. Neither group offered a word.

Verl watched them enter the house, and his eyes were sad. This was the breaking up of a family, and he hated to think that he was the cause.

"I'm sorry, Pa," he said. "I guess I lost my head. But when I saw Kale mishandling Jigger, all I wanted to do was to get at him."

Jabez stared toward the house, and Verl wondered what tormented thoughts ran through his mind. Did Jabez regret his action in telling the twins to leave? Would he like to recall those words?

Owen spoke first. "I don't feel any sorrow. This has

been building up for a long while. I say we're lucky the break happened without somebody getting seriously hurt. Pa, I think one of us better go into the house and check on what they're taking. I wouldn't put it past those two to steal us blind."

"You're too hard on them, Owen," Jabez muttered. "They've got a lot of faults, but they're not thieves."

"Not that you know of," Owen retorted.

Jabez shook himself, as though trying to throw off a bad memory. "Well, it's done. Sure, I'm sorry. But I wouldn't change it if I had the chance. They've been on our backs almost since the day they were born. Don't be blaming yourself, Verl. Me, I'm just damned glad it's over."

Verl's expression showed his relief. At least Jabez wasn't accusing him of this breakup. "Me and Owen will move those cattle, Pa."

"Both of you take your rifles," Jabez warned.

At their surprised looks, he said, "I'm not saying they'd go that far to get even. But with the twisted way they look at things, I'm not certain what might happen."

"If it'll make you any easier, Pa, we'll take the rifles," Verl said.

"I'm telling you one thing," Owen burst out. "We're not leaving until we see them ride out. Damn it, you don't think we'd go and leave you alone while those two are here."

Jabez started to protest and held it. "All right, boys," he agreed. "If it'll make you feel any better."

Owen thought of their interrupted breakfast. "Pa, could those hotcakes be rewarmed?"

Jabez's grin was steady enough. "Doesn't make any difference. I can make new ones."

Chapter Five

Kyle twisted in the saddle to look back at the house. "Not a damned one of them even bothered to see us off," he complained.

"Is the little boy scared of being away from home?" Kale jeered.

Kyle whipped around toward his brother. His eyes were furious. "Don't you go wiping that mouth on me, Kale Wakeman. I won't stand for it."

"Sure, Kyle," Kale said soothingly. "I was just trying to be funny."

"At my expense," Kyle grumbled. He glanced at the hoofs of his brother's mount. The horse's stride seemed normal. "I thought you said your horse was almost lame," he said. He was still angry at Kale's jeering remark.

Kale's laugh was an ugly burst of sound. "I just told Verl that. I wanted to use Jigger. I never got to before. Verl was so damned particular about him." Thinking of Verl released a string of oaths. "Verl's never going to forget this day," he finished.

That erased all of Kyle's rancor. Both of them had suffered at Verl's hands. "What will we do about it, Kale?"

Kale frowned. "We don't have to rush it. Right now, I'm thinking about what we're going to do. This is a bad time of year to be looking for work. I don't know of anybody hiring now."

Kyle wanted to ask Kale if he was scared, and decided against it. "I've got four dollars and some change, Kale."

"And I've got nearly eight. That'll keep us for a few

days until something turns up. Damn it," he muttered. "Staying alive could raise some problems."

Ah, Kyle thought in triumph. If he isn't scared, he's worried. It's about the same thing. They rode a good ten minutes before Kyle dared ask cautiously: "You sorry we left, Kale?"

Kale spit into the road. "I'd be just as satisfied never to see that place again."

Kyle guessed Kale was tougher than he was. He couldn't stop that uneasy hollow in his stomach. He didn't care what Kale said. He felt lonely. For the first time in his life he didn't have the comforts of a home to bolster him, or a sense of belonging somewhere.

"Something bothering you, Kyle?"

"Yes," Kyle confessed. "I can't help wondering what we're going to do, where we're going. It'd be nice to be a Kid Curry. He's got Butch Cassidy behind him."

Kale winked at him. "I've been thinking the same thing."

Kyle remembered how pleasant Butch Cassidy had been to them, of the drinks he had bought, refusing to let the twins return the favor. He shook his head. That was wistful thinking.

"You don't think much of the idea?" Kale asked caustically.

"It's not that," Kyle protested. "But why should Cassidy take us in? We couldn't do him any good."

Kale's eyes were aflame with a new interest. "Not right now," he admitted. "But maybe we can change that."

He had something in mind all right, but despite Kyle's prodding, he refused to answer any further questions. "You'll see," was Kale's only response.

Kyle had to leave it at that. Kale had always been the leader. Kyle had been content to follow.

"Where are we going now, Kale?"

"We need money, don't we?" Kale asked practically. "What we've got won't last long. We're going to stop by and see Etta." At the flash of apprehension in Kyle's eyes, he asked, "Does that bother you?"

"I was thinking of what Owen said. He warned you to stay away from her."

31

Kale spit again, and it was a scornful answer. "If that's worrying you, Owen won't be in town today. He and Verl will be moving those cattle for Pa." He grinned at Kyle's explosive puff of breath. "Thought that would ease your mind."

Kyle found himself humming as he rode along. He should have had more belief in Kale. He couldn't remember a time when Kale had let him down. Damned if it wasn't funny how a man's moods could lift or depress him. A moment ago, he had been worried about the future. There was no solution at the moment, but somehow Kyle knew everything was going to be all right.

Neither of them spoke the remaining distance to South Pass City. South Pass was a twenty-mile gap in the Divide. At one time, hordes of migrant trains had toiled through the gap, but that migration had tailed off the past few years. South Pass City would be almost deserted, if it hadn't been for the outlaws that poured into the town during the winter months. The weather cut down their activities, and South Pass City was about as good as any other town to ride out the dull days. Maybe even better, for the law was weak there and showed no inclination to pry into the outlaws' doings.

Kyle didn't see anybody they knew as they rode down the main street. Occasionally they passed groups of men, soaking up the strengthening sun. Kyle felt a small throb of excitement as he wondered if those men could be outlaws. He thought enviously of the deference with which Cassidy and Curry were regarded. Maybe someday he and Kale would have the same standing.

Kale and Kyle pulled up before a small, weatherbeaten house on the outskirts of the city. It was a tired house, showing its age. There wasn't much attempt to keep up with the increasing need of repairs. The Faber girls' father was a sickly man, pretty badly crippled up with rheumatism. He had been a miner in his prime years, and some said that Cleatis had struck it rich. Kyle judged the house with a critical eye. Maybe not rich, he thought. Rich people wouldn't pick a house like this to live in. But old Cleatis must have managed to save a little money, for he no longer worked, and as far as Kyle knew, neither Etta nor Ann worked. Living money had to come from someplace.

He swung down and joined Kale and moved up the walk to the front porch. He was always uneasy when he was here. There was always the chance Owen would come along and find them here. He didn't think Ann Faber cared much for either him or Kale, and Cleatis was always abrupt. If he wasn't complaining about his aching joints, he sat there a-weighing in his eyes. Etta was a different matter. Her enthusiasm showed every time she saw Kale.

"You let me do the talking," Kale said before he knocked.

Etta answered the knock, and her pleasure at seeing Kale showed in her squeal of joy.

"Kale," she cried. "It seems like a year since I last saw you." Her face turned reproachful. "I'd begun thinking you'd forgotten all about me."

"You know better than that," Kale retorted. He hugged her hard. "Does that show how glad I am to see you again?"

Kyle swallowed. Damn, but Kale was daring. Kyle didn't like to think what would happen if old Cleatis came in and saw that hug.

But Etta liked it. Her face was a rosy red and there was no reproach in her manner or words. "It'll do for a start," she replied pertly. "Come in, come in. Can I get you something?"

Kale held her hand as they walked into the parlor. Kyle didn't know how old Etta was, but he thought somewhere near his and Kale's age. She was small but sweetly made, and her shining blondness was a foil for Kale's darkness. They were alike in nature too, Kyle mused. She had an impulsiveness that matched Kale's. Kyle remembered the afternoon last fall when she had borrowed his horse and raced Kale down the main street. She didn't win, but she had pressed Kale hard. Etta and Kale would get along just fine, if Owen wasn't constantly interfering.

"Did you mean that about getting us something?" Kale asked.

"You know I did, Kale."

33

"If you've got a few crusts of bread for a couple of hungry traveling men, we'd sure appreciate it," Kale said easily. "We didn't get any breakfast this morning."

"Why, that's awful," Etta exclaimed. "Sit down. I'll be right back." She whirled and hurried out of the room.

Kale and Kyle sat down in the small parlor. Kale winked at his brother, and the wink was a boast in itself. Kyle's eyes roamed about the room. It was shabbily furnished, and the wallpaper was faded and dirty. This place wasn't any better than the place he and Kale had left this morning. He didn't see how Etta was going to do them any good, but Kale had something in mind. Kale looked almost happy, and that was rare.

"She likes you," Kyle said cautiously. That was a personal matter, and he might be stepping on Kale's toes. One could never tell just how Kale would turn.

"She'd be my girl, if it wasn't for that damned Owen," Kale said.

Kyle's eyes were round. "Has she said so?"

"No, but I know. A man gets to know such things."

Kyle whistled soundlessly. "Didn't Owen find her first?"

Kale nodded complacently. "He introduced me to her." He glared at Kyle. "Do you think that gives him some sort of a settler's right? He's got no permanent brand on her."

"How does she feel, Kale?"

"Haven't talked to her yet. I will one of these days."

Kyle was sorry Etta returned to the room at the moment. Kale was more talkative than usual, and Kyle was curious.

Etta carried a plate of sandwiches in one hand, a pot of coffee in the other. "I've got to go back and get cups," she said. "You can start on this. They're only roast beef."

Kyle's stomach rumbled as he reached for a sandwich. Etta shouldn't downgrade this food.

Kale said it better. "You're an angel from heaven, Etta."

"Oh, you," she said flippantly, but her face showed how pleased she was.

34

Etta came back with the cups and poured the coffee. She looked at the plate, and half of the sandwiches were gone. "You two were hungry," she remarked.

Kale grinned. "Did you think I was lying to you?"

She smiled at him. "I don't think you would dare."

The two were lost in a shared moment, but Kyle was worrying. At any instant, Cleatis could walk into the room. Kyle wasn't sure how he would react at finding the Wakeman twins eating in his house, but Kyle had the uneasy feeling it wouldn't be favorably. "Isn't your pa home?" he asked.

Etta shook her head. "He went out about an hour ago. With the sunshine, his joints move a little easier. He thought he'd take a short stroll downtown and see if any of his old friends were around."

Kyle sighed. That was one big worry gone. A small one was left. Ann didn't approve of either him or Kale. She never put it into words, but her reserved attitude was eloquent enough.

"Isn't Ann here?" he asked.

"She went with Pa to see that he got along all right. I don't expect them back for some time."

Kyle could relax and enjoy the moment. He poured himself another cup of coffee, reached for another sandwich, then settled back.

"You've got some questions to answer, Mr. Kale," Etta announced. "What did you mean when you said you were traveling men? And why didn't you eat breakfast?"

Kale's face turned sad and mournful. "It's a sad story, Etta. You know Owen objects to me coming here." He waited for Etta's nod. "Well, Owen built up his unhappiness about it with a lot of lies to Verl. Verl went to Pa. He finally convinced Pa, and Pa ordered us off the place."

Etta was tight-lipped. She didn't doubt a word Kale said. "I never did care for Verl. He always was too bossy."

"He is that," Kale agreed solemnly.

Kyle was chortling inside. That damned Kale was a clever one. He took partial truths, weaved them in with

35

some downright lies, and came up with a plausible story that bore inspection.

"What are you going to do, Kale?" Etta asked.

Kale twisted at his hands. "It's a problem, Etta. Bad time of the year to be out of work. Nobody hiring. But Kyle and me worked out a deal that's going to do all right for us." His face grew long and mournful again. "The only trouble is that we're short of money. Without money, there goes our deal."

Etta was thoughtful for a moment. "How much would you need?"

"It wouldn't take much," Kale mused.

Etta rose. "Let me see how much money there is in the house."

"Golly, Etta, I wasn't trying to get money from you. I just wanted you to know how it is."

"Don't you think I'm interested in you?" she retorted. "If a little money will pull off your deal, then I'd be happy to furnish it."

She walked out of the room, her steps purposeful.

Kale winked at Kyle. Kyle stared at him in awe. That Kale was getting to be the damnedest liar.

Etta was gone a few minutes, then returned, her face radiant. She held out some bills and said: "That's all there is in the house. I hope it's enough."

Kale counted the money. "Thirty-four dollars." His voice held a jubilant note. "I think this will do it, Etta." He shook his head fiercely. "But I can't take this money from you. What if the deal falls through?"

"It won't," she said firmly.

"Well, all right," Kale said weakly. "But it's only a loan. I promise to get this money back to you."

"I'm not worried," she said brightly.

Kyle swallowed hard to keep his words from pouring out. He didn't know what Kale had in mind, but he knew one thing: Kale was going to have to return the money, or he would lose his standing with Etta.

Kale stuffed the money into his pocket. "You've saved our lives, Etta. I don't know what we would have done without you."

She started to answer, when Ann came into the room. She was several years older than her sister, and she didn't have Etta's flaming spirit. Kyle knew Verl was interested in Ann. As for him, he would pick Etta over her sister every time.

Ann's dark eyes went from Kale to Kyle, and her manner was quiet and reserved. She was always that way when she was around the twins. She didn't have to say she didn't like them. It stuck out all over her.

"Hello, Kale, Kyle," Ann said. "What are you doing here?"

Kyle waited anxiously. He instinctively knew Ann would explode if she heard about Etta giving them the money. Kale must have sensed it too, for there was a warning in the glance he gave Etta.

"Do you know what's happened?" Etta burst out indignantly. "Verl told Mr. Wakeman a lot of lies about the twins. Verl got Kale and Kyle kicked out."

Ann's penetrating gaze went from Kale to Kyle before she looked back at Etta. "I don't believe it," she said flatly.

"It's true, Ann," Kale said lugubriously. "We couldn't make Pa listen to us. It happened just the way Etta said."

Ann was vigorously shaking her head. "There's something more behind this. I know Verl. He doesn't lie."

Kale lifted his hands and let them fall helplessly. "I can't help it if you don't believe me," he said sadly.

Etta was furious and she tore into Ann. "Don't you call Kale a liar," she snapped. "You've always had your highhanded way. I'm getting sick of it."

"Wait a minute, Etta," Kale remonstrated. "I don't want you sisters falling out because of something that happened to us."

Etta couldn't be appeased. "She's always been like this," she said petulantly. "She never tries to find out what actually happened."

Ann's face was stiff with shock at her sister's outrage, but she offered no protest.

"I think we'd better go, Etta," Kale said.

"I'll see you again, Kale?" Etta's eyes were anxious.

"You know you will," he replied heartily. "I've got to let you know how things turn out, don't I?"

Etta came to the front door with them. Kale squeezed her hands. "Everything's going to turn out all right. You'll see."

Chapter Six

Kale grinned maliciously as he swung up into the saddle. He looked toward the house and said: "There's going to be a hell of a row in there. I'll bet it's going on right now."

The possible quarrel between sisters didn't bother Kyle. He was concerned with a more practical matter. "Kale, how are we going to get that money back to Etta?" A suspicion crossed his mind. "Or do you intend to return it?"

"Hell, yes, I intend to return it. You don't think I'd let Etta down, do you?"

"You just tell me how we're going to do it?" Kyle argued.

"Keep your mouth shut and your eyes open," Kale growled. "You'll learn something."

Kyle subsided into a sulky silence. Sometimes, Kale got on his nerves.

He didn't ask any questions as he followed Kale back to the business district of town. His curiosity rose again as Kale stopped at Creed Dawson's gun shop. Kyle knew who Dawson was, but he'd never been in his store. He had no reason to do any business with him.

Kyle swung down and joined Kale. "What are we doing here, Kale?"

"*You've* got a gun," Kale pointed out. "*I* haven't."

"Owen said he'd leave it at Sanderson's store the next time he came into town."

Kale snorted. "I haven't got time to waste waiting on him. I'm hoping old Creed has something I can afford."

A tall, lanky man dozed behind the counter. He was almost completely bald, and even in the subdued light of the shop there was a shine to his head.

"Hello, Creed," Kale said loudly.

Dawson glanced at them in annoyance as though he didn't appreciate being awakened. He stood and asked indifferently, "What do you two want?" The Wakeman twins belonged to what was called the respectable class. Dawson never expected any business from their kind.

"Thought we'd see what you've got in the way of a cheap gun, Creed," Kale replied.

Dawson's face showed more interest. The Wakemans had lived around here long enough to know the people with whom he dealt. Dawson's business came from the Wild Bunch and others of their kind.

"You sure you're in the right place?" he asked carefully.

"I think I am," Kale replied easily. "I'm tired of wearing my ass to the bone without getting anything for it. I figure it's about time I start collecting some of what I figure's owed me."

Dawson grinned, displaying bad teeth. This was the way most of the outlaws started out. A young kid grew weary of having empty pockets and planned to do something about the lack of money. They thought the world owed them a living. Dawson had seen scores of young ones get cut down before they even began collecting what they thought was due them.

"You sure you know what you're doing?" he asked.

"You let *us* worry about that," Kale snapped. "What have you got in the way of guns?"

Dawson shrugged. He had gone as far as he could. This was their affair. These two were the rankest of newcomers, and Dawson could have told them of the overpowering percentage of amateurs who never made their second attempt to get rich quick. But it was no skin off his nose. He reached into a display case, pulled out several guns, and laid them before Kale.

Kale winced at the price Dawson put on them.

"We haven't got a gold mine in our pockets," Kale snapped. "Have you got anything cheaper?"

Dawson didn't grin, though he wanted to. He didn't

know what these two had in mind, but whatever it was, it was going to be started on a shoestring.

"How about one of these?" Dawson asked and pulled out several older-looking guns.

Kale scowled as he inspected the weapons. They had seen a lot of service and were pretty badly beaten. Most of the bluing had worn off the barrels, and the butts showed nicks and scratches.

"Do these damned things shoot?" Kale asked.

Dawson looked injured. His trade might be questionable, but nobody ever questioned his handicraft. He was a top gunsmith and proud of the fact.

"I worked every one of them over myself," he said stiffly. "They'll do everything you want."

"You don't know what I want," Kale said and grinned wickedly. He aimed the muzzle directly at Dawson's head.

"Put that damned thing down," Dawson said icily. "Proves you haven't been around guns as much as you want people to think." His eyes were angry, but otherwise his face was unperturbed. "Besides, that gun isn't loaded. I learned long ago never to keep a loaded gun in the shop."

Kale slowly lowered the gun, and his strident cackle rang out. "What's the matter? Did you think I was going to shoot you?"

"I never know what a fool kid will do," Dawson growled. He was suddenly weary of both the Wakemans. "Do you want to buy a gun or not?"

The snap in his voice put a heated flush in Kale's face. "You're kinda rough on your customers, aren't you?" he complained.

"Only when they ask for it," Dawson snapped. He reached for the gun in Kale's hand. This fool kid wasn't going to buy anything.

"Wait a minute," Kale objected. "I'm not through looking at it."

"I haven't got all day to stand here. Do you want it or not?"

Kale couldn't meet the piercing impact of Dawson's eyes. "I guess I'll take it," he said in a surly tone. "Will you throw in a couple of boxes of cartridges?"

"At a price," Dawson said. "I'm giving you a good price on that gun, and you know it."

"It's a deal," Kale said. He counted out twenty dollars of the money Etta had given him.

"Want me to wrap it up?" Dawson asked.

"Hell, no," Kale stated. "I'm going to carry it." He dropped the gun into his sheepskin pocket. He reached for the boxes of shells, but Dawson's hand covered them before Kale could touch them.

"You only paid for the gun," he said pointedly.

Kale grumbled while he shelled out two more bills. "You don't go out of your way to be obliging," he said petulantly.

Dawson grinned frostily. "If I went your way, I'd be out of business in a hurry. Anything else?"

"This will do," Kale said shortly. He walked to the door, and Kyle followed him. Neither one saw Dawson shake his head.

"Why did you buy that?" Kyle asked when they got outside.

"Because I needed it," Kale said shortly.

"But it took most of the money Etta loaned you." Kyle's eyes widened. "You don't intend to pay her back."

Kale flushed. He didn't like anybody questioning his word. "I said I'd pay her back, didn't I?"

Kyle frowned puzzledly. "I don't see how that gun is going to do us any good."

"You would, if you used your head. I'm tired of getting along on the occasional dollar somebody throws our way. I'm going to get it my way, a lot of it."

Kyle choked as the realization of what Kale meant sank into his mind. "You mean you're going to rob somebody?"

Kale grinned wolfishly. "I was kinda thinking along those lines."

"Just what lines are those?" Kyle demanded.

"There's plenty of stagecoaches running through this country," Kale said easily. "The right stage could set us up on Easy Street."

Kyle groaned softly. "Hell, Kale. They'll run you down. The law can get a line on you by going straight to

41

Dawson's. Dawson will tell the law you bought a gun in there."

Kale spat in disgust. "Creed will never open his mouth. He doesn't dare. Most of his business comes from outlaws."

He saw that Kyle was still unconvinced, and his voice picked up a harsher note. "How do you think Cassidy and Curry got their start? The same way we're doing. We can work our way up to something big. Maybe even big enough to make Cassidy notice us. Damn it, he might even invite us to join him. How does that sound?"

Kyle shook his head hopelessly. Kale could always make things sound so good.

Kale's face hardened. "Are you in or out? You can go back and beg Pa to take you back. If you beg hard enough, you might get him to listen. Then he could kick your ass around from now on. Make up your mind. In or out?"

A shiver ran through Kyle, and it wasn't solely due to the sharpness of the breeze. He and Kale had never been separated in anything. He couldn't bear the thought of separation now. "I guess I'm in," he said weakly.

Kale slapped him on the shoulder. "Knew you would see it that way."

Chapter Seven

Kyle was in a complaining mood as he and Kale sat beside the road that was just beginning to dry out. This spot was only a few miles out of Rawlins, and Kyle had complained all the way here.

"Why did you pick this spot?" he demanded.

"For God's sake, will you shut up. Lots of traffic between Rawlins and Casper. If I'm right, a stagecoach should be along anytime now."

"At least you accomplished something on your trip to Rawlins," Kyle said bitterly. Kale had had another night living in town. He still resented having to sleep outside while Kale went into town to look things over.

Kale glared at him. "Will you quit your bellyaching. I told you why both of us didn't go in. Seeing a couple of strangers could be a tipoff that something was brewing."

"But you slept in a bed," Kyle said in a sulky tone. "And you ate your meals in a restaurant." Last night was one of the coldest nights he had ever spent. He had crawled into a shallow cave that turned the wind, but it had been no barrier against the cold. Kyle had shivered and suffered all through the night.

Kale was furious. "I ate one meal in a restaurant. I brought you some food."

"Cold food," Kyle said in an injured tone.

"Oh, goddamn it," Kale swore. "I almost wish you hadn't agreed to throw in with me. All you've done is bellyache. If it makes you feel any better, I didn't sleep in a hotel bed. I didn't want some hotel clerk remembering me. I burrowed into a haystack outside of town."

That partially mollified Kyle. Kale hadn't had it easy, either. He looked at the ground and muttered: "I wish that damned stage would come along. I want to get this over." Their horses were tethered a hundred yards off the road in a dense copse. Kale had picked this spot halfway up the long, steep grade. A coach would have to slow down before it climbed the grade.

Kale threw up a hand for attention. "I think I hear a coach coming. Put on your mask. I'll take the other side of the road. Watch yourself. I don't know how many will be traveling on the coach, or how well armed they are. They might put up some resistance."

A shiver of apprehension ran through Kyle. For the first time, he was thinking of how dangerous this business could be. If those travelers decided to shoot back, Kyle Wakeman could be the target.

He gulped as he tied in place the crude mask Kale had fashioned out of a bandanna. He wondered if Kale was suffering such tremors.

Kyle stood behind a small tree, miserably waiting. If he had a choice right now between his former life and this one, he would go back gladly.

The hoofbeats sounded louder. Kyle glanced hastily across the road. Kale had hidden himself well. Kyle could catch only a glimpse of him.

The coach came into view a good way down the road. The driver was applying the whip, trying to get all the momentum he could before he tackled the grade.

Kyle ached with tension. This was his first real attempt to break the law. Oh, he had committed some minor misdeeds, kid stuff. But this was serious. This one act was going to take him and Kale out of the safe life they knew and put the whole world against them.

Kyle heard Kale's soft whistle, a mere whisper of sound. It warned Kyle to be ready.

The coach slammed into the grade, and the steepness immediately began taking its toll. The wheels slowed, and the horses began to labor. Their speed rapidly fell off. Halfway up the hill they were barely walking.

Kale picked the exact moment to step out into the road. He leveled a pistol at the driver and barked, "Hold it, right there."

Kyle stepped out on the other side of the road. He wasn't shaking now. It was only the anticipation of the moment that was bad. Now that it was here he felt only excitement.

"Better do what he said." Kyle's voice was calm and measured.

The driver whipped his head from Kale to Kyle, and his face froze. He stood as he hauled on the reins, pulling the horses to a stop. The horses stood, tossing their heads, throwing great gobs of foam with each toss. Their hoofs still danced nervously, but they didn't fight the drag of the reins.

"You picked the wrong stage this time," the driver said. His voice wasn't quite steady.

"We'll be the judge of that," Kale snapped. "Tell your passengers to get out."

The driver raised his voice. "It's a holdup. Get out. Take it easy. Nobody will get hurt."

"Now you're showing some smart," Kale approved.

Three men climbed out of the stage, their hands upraised, their eyes rolling. Two of them were dressed in the rough clothes of working ranchmen; the third one wore the fancy clothes of a city man, even to the round, hard hat. He was trembling so hard that Kyle wondered how his legs supported him.

"Stay where you are," Kale ordered the driver, "and hold that stage in place." A thought occurred to him, and he said, "Throw down your wallet."

Kyle came around the stage and joined Kale. That driver was a cool one. He showed no undue signs of haste. He pulled his wallet from his hip pocket and tossed it on the ground. "Won't be worth your time to go through it," he remarked.

"See what he's got," Kale ordered.

Kyle picked up the wallet. He went through it, and his voice showed his disappointment. "Only three dollars." He gulped back the remainder of his words. He had almost called out Kale's name.

Kale was furious at Kyle's announcement. "Goddamn you, I ought to shoot you," he raved at the driver.

"Go ahead," the driver said easily. "It'll go harder on you."

Kyle had to admire the driver. He never lost his head. His eyes were intent on the two holdup men, as though trying to memorize every detail about them.

"See what the others have," Kale ordered.

None of the passengers showed any signs of resistance. Kyle went from one passenger to another. He chortled with pleasure as he went through the wallets of the men in rough clothes. He didn't take time to count the money, but his hands were filled with bills. He stuffed them into his pocket, then approached the city dude.

"Don't shoot me," the man begged. He was so terrified that his teeth clicked together, and slobber ran down his chin.

It gave Kyle a heady sense of power to have this much authority. "Shut your damned mouth," he snarled. "Hand over your wallet."

45

He took the wallet from the man's shaking hand. He opened it and almost whooped his delight. "It's stuffed with money." Again, he almost said Kale's name.

"Good," Kale said. "See what they've got in their suitcases."

The two ranchers shook their heads. They weren't traveling with any luggage. The city man had two pieces of luggage, a valise and a large, flat case.

Kyle went through them. "Nothing in this one but some fancy city clothes," he remarked.

"What's in the other one?" Kale asked impatiently.

Kyle opened the flat case and whistled. "I'll be damned. Nothing but women's dresses."

"I'm a traveling salesman," the city man babbled. "That's my sample case."

Kale looked down over Kyle's shoulder at the opened case. "Hey, some of those dresses look pretty fancy. We'll take the case."

"You can't do that," the salesman squalled. "That's the way I make my living."

Kale thrust his pistol at him. "Would you rather be dead?"

The salesman shrank back against the coach, his face going pale.

Kyle snapped the case shut and stood.

Kale motioned to the driver with the pistol. "Tell them to get back in. Get going. If you even think of trying to stop, I'll blow you off that seat."

"Climb back in," the driver advised his passengers. "We ain't arguing with you two." He gave them a long, thoughtful look before he released the brakes and snapped the reins over the team's backs.

The horses plodded up the remainder of the grade, then the stage lurched forward as it climbed to the crest.

Kale watched the stage disappear out of sight. "Didn't take them long to get out of here, did it?" he asked and chortled.

"How much do you think we got, Kale?" Kyle asked eagerly. "I didn't count it, but it looks like a big haul."

"We don't stop here to count it," Kale said scathingly. "We'll do the counting when we're a long way from here."

46

They rode for a good two miles before Kale condescended to stop. He picked a thick growth of trees and rode into it.

He dismounted and jerked the makeshift mask from his face. "Easy, wasn't it?" he remarked.

"A lot easier than I thought it would be," Kyle confessed.

"How much did we make?" Kale asked impatiently.

Kyle pulled money from one pocket. "I put what I got from the ranchers in here." He counted rapidly and shook his head in disappointment. "Less than I thought. It's all in dollar bills. Twenty-seven dollars. The driver's money adds three more."

Kale was disappointed too, for he swore fluently. "How much did you get from the drummer?"

Kyle's face grew more rapt as he counted, and his breathing came faster. "A hundred and sixty-four dollars," he said unbelievingly.

"Selling women dresses must pay pretty good," Kale said.

That reminded Kyle of something. "What are you going to do with the drummer's dress case, Kale?"

Kale winked at him. "When I saw them, I thought of Etta. She'd look pretty good in them, wouldn't she?"

Kyle hated to dampen Kale's enthusiasm, but he had to point out some things. "If they fit. And if somebody doesn't see her wearing them and connects them to this robbery."

"South Pass City is quite a way from where we took this stuff," Kale said. "Nobody will connect them."

He was lost in thought, and Kyle dared venture, "Do you plan on returning Etta's loan?"

"Sure I do," Kale retorted impatiently. "I was just thinking of what we're going to do next."

"Have you thought of anything yet?" Kyle asked. No longer did he doubt his brother. Look how well this had gone off. Kale had a brain in his head, and he used it.

"Something far bigger, Kyle. Stagecoaches are too slow. At this rate, it'd take a thousand holdups to make any real money."

Kyle felt the excitement stir in him. "Where's that real money?"

"On a train," Kale said promptly. "A train robber would catch Cassidy's eye. He'd know we're important enough to consider when we ask to join him."

Chapter Eight

Sam Travis dismounted before the Wakemans' house as though every joint ached. Each successive winter was harder to get through. It was due to increasing age, and he could do nothing about that.

He hallooed the house. "Anybody home?"

He waited for a response, his shoulders drooping. He looked the picture of weary dejection.

Verl came to the door. "Hello, Sam," he greeted. "What pulls you out this way?"

"Business," Travis answered sourly. "Seems like a man can't get a moment's peace any more."

Verl hid his grin. Travis might have been an efficient sheriff some years ago. Looking at this sagging figure, it was hard to believe that he had ever been young and ambitious.

"Come in and have a cup of coffee," he invited.

"Sounds good," Travis grunted. "I think this is the worst time of year, Verl. The promise of spring is here, but her teeth are still sharp. Damned wind cuts right through a man."

"You made only one mistake, Sam," Verl said gravely.

"What's that?" Travis asked in mild surprise.

Verl chuckled. "You shouldn't have gotten old."

"Don't I know it,' Travis replied fervently.

He walked into the kitchen where Jabez and Owen were seated at the table. They greeted him effusively, for Travis was a likable man.

Travis shook hands with each of them, then said, "Jabez, I don't see enough of you any more."

"I don't get around very much, Sam," Jabez answered quietly.

"I know it," Travis replied. "It's my fault I don't get out here more often. But you know how it is." He made a vague gesture and offered no further explanation.

Verl poured him a cup of coffee, and Travis drained half of it in a single swallow. "That goes straight to my cold, old bones," he said with satisfaction. "I can feel the ice melting from around them."

Verl refilled the cup. "I can lace that with a shot of whiskey, Sam."

"Tempting," Travis grunted. "But maybe I better pass it by now. I'm here on official business."

That statement raised three pairs of eyebrows.

Owen recovered first. He grinned and said, "I knew we were pretty bad, Sam, but I didn't think it'd come to official attention yet."

Travis managed a frosty grin. "If they were all like you people, I wouldn't be pulled out of my office on a raw day like this. There was a stagecoach robbery just outside of Rawlins yesterday."

That wiped the grin off Owen's face, and he leaned forward, his face intent. "Do you think we had something to do with that, Sam?" There was no resentment in his voice. "None of us have been near Rawlins for months. Hell, maybe years."

"I know that," Travis said gruffly. "I was just out here to pick up some information, if it's available." He was silent a moment, his brow furrowed in thought.

"Since the Wild Bunch has been wintering at South Pass City, I didn't think you had any trouble like that," Verl said.

Travis flushed at the implication. It was pretty well known that an unwritten agreement existed between the lawless men and the authorities.

"The Wild Bunch didn't pull this robbery," Travis growled.

"You know that for sure?" Verl insisted.

"As damned sure as I can get, Verl. I rode over to

Rawlins and talked to the victims. It was an amateur job, done by only two men. It wasn't a big haul, less than two hundred dollars was taken. The Wild Bunch plan their robberies more carefully than that. They wouldn't stir out for a piddling little job like that."

He drummed on the tabletop with his fingertips. Something was bothering him, and he didn't know quite how to put it.

"Why don't you just go ahead and tell us about it," Jabez suggested.

Travis still hesitated, then his words poured out. "Somebody told me the twins haven't been here for the past three or four days."

Verl stiffened as he caught the implication in the statement. Good God! The twins wouldn't be so foolish as to do something like that.

Jabez missed the threat in Travis' statement. "They haven't been here. I kicked them off. Told 'em I didn't want to see them back."

"Any particular reason?" Travis asked softly.

"Family quarrel," Jabez returned stiffly.

That was no lie, Verl thought. Jabez wouldn't want to talk about the quarrel that had split the family. But Travis had some purpose in asking about the twins. "Why did you want to know about them, Sam?"

Travis sighed. He had known and liked these people for a long time, and if possible, he wanted to avoid hurting them. His eyes were fastened on the table as he said: "I told you only two men held up the stage. I asked for descriptions. What I got was pretty sketchy. The two were masked with red bandannas with eyeholes cut out. You know how unreliable eyewitnesses can be. One man sees things one way, another an entirely different way."

"And your witnesses varied?" Verl said.

"They sure as hell did," Travis answered mournfully. "Two ranchers and a salesman were on that stage. They disagreed on everything. Two of them said the holdup men were tall and skinny. The salesman said both of them were short and fat."

Verl got a glimpse of what Travis had been driving

at. Travis had an idea lodged in his mind that the twins were involved.

"That kinda clears the twins, doesn't it?" he asked.

Travis doggedly shook his head. "It might have, except for the driver. He's been driving stages for a lot of years. He's trained himself to notice details. He said the two men were of identical height and about the same weight. If he could have seen their faces, he said he would bet he was looking at twins. Funny he used that term," Travis finished reflectively.

Verl felt as though all the air was jolted out of him. Across the table Jabez was spluttering, and Owen looked stunned.

"Were the two holdup men armed?" Verl asked carefully.

"Both of them. The driver spoke with emphasis about the way they waved pistols around. He said he'd looked down enough of those barrels to make him puke."

Verl leaned back in his chair, suddenly relieved. "It couldn't have been Kale and Kyle," he said slowly. "Kale didn't have a gun when he left here. Owen told him he'd take it into town and leave it at Sanderson's. The gun's still here. Owen hasn't been to town yet."

"Sam, don't you try to tell me they could have bought a pistol," Jabez yelled. "They only had a few dollars between them. You tell me where they got the money."

"Jabez, that doesn't prove a damned thing," Travis said sorrowfully. "And you know it. They could have bought a pistol from Dawson. He's got pistols at all prices. I don't know how Kale and Kyle would have worked it, but it could have been done."

Verl scowled at him. "Are you accusing Kale and Kyle, Sam?"

Travis shook his head. "No," he said stubbornly. "I'm just pointing out how it could have been them. A lot of signs are beginning to point their way. I've got to go along with those signs until I know they're leading me wrong."

"Dawson sells guns only at his price," Verl snapped. "You tell me where Kale and Kyle got their hands on

51

the money to buy anything from Dawson. Have you asked Dawson if the twins were in his shop?"

Travis finished his coffee, shook his head at Verl's offer of a refill, and stood. "I have. Dawson just stared at me blank-faced. He claims he doesn't even know the twins."

"I'm saying he's a damned liar," Verl argued. "If he lies about one thing, he'll lie about another. The twins have been around long enough for Dawson to know them."

Travis eyed him speculatively. "You arguing *against* or *for* your brothers?"

"I'm just saying Dawson is a liar," Verl said levelly. "Everybody knows where most of his business comes from. If he sold that gun to someone, he would never name him. Dawson knows which side his bread's buttered on. I'm saying you're looking for the wrong men when you set out after Kale and Kyle."

Travis shook his head, completely unconvinced. "I'm not saying you're wrong, Verl. And not right, either. I have to convince myself. Where are the twins right now?"

That helpless look returned to Verl's face. "I told you they left a few days ago," he said hotly. "I don't know where they are. Damned if you're not a hard head, Sam."

"Maybe," Travis agreed politely. "But until I get definite proof one way or the other, I've got to go where my nose points." He walked to the door and stopped there. "If you do see Kale or Kyle, you better point out what damned fools they could be. One success leads to a hunger for another. When kids get on this track, there's usually only one way to stop them. I'll keep in touch with you." He looked at each face in turn, nodded, and closed the door behind him.

Jabez broke the silence after Travis left. "That's just damned guesswork," he raved. "Those boys wouldn't do something like that." He looked appealingly at Verl. "You don't think they would, do you, Verl?"

"I don't know a damned thing about them," Verl said unhappily. "We lost all hold on them when they left. I know one thing for sure. I'm going to talk to Creed

52

Dawson, or beat the truth out of him. We'll know, one way or the other, if the twins are involved."

"You know better than that, Verl," Owen stated. "Nobody can make Creed talk if he doesn't want to."

Verl looked at his father. Jabez looked sick. "We'll see," he muttered.

Chapter Nine

After three long days, Kyle was weary of riding. They had visited several towns, and Kyle couldn't see where they were getting anyplace.

"Kale, what good is all this riding doing us?"

Kale frowned at him. "I'm trying to find the right spot. We're not going to rush into anything until I see how the ground lays."

Kyle sighed. Nothing was going to turn Kale when he made up his mind. "What's this town ahead of us?"

"Wilcox," Kale answered. "This may be the spot I'm looking for."

"Why here?" Kyle argued.

"They make up trains at Wilcox. The town we're looking for may be right here."

The proximity of possible action worried Kyle. "Kale, do you think just the two of us can handle it? Robbing a train's a big job."

"Hell, yes, we can handle it. That's why I bought the dynamite in Rock Springs."

Just the mention of dynamite increased Kyle's worry. "Kale, do you know enough about dynamite to handle it?"

"I know." Kale sounded positive enough. "You may have forgotten six years ago I helped Verl blow out some rock to open up that creek on the home place. I didn't know when I would ever want to use it, but I watched him good." He reached back and patted a saddlebag. "You're going to be damned glad I did."

Kyle moaned deep in his throat. He had thrown in with his brother, and he couldn't see any way of backing out now. "I just hope to God you know what you're doing," he said fervently.

Kale grinned at him. "I know."

Wilcox was a small town on the Union Pacific track that ran from Cheyenne to Casper. Kale and Kyle rode through the town, Kale's eyes constantly darting about him. Kyle didn't have the slightest idea of what he was looking for.

Kale stopped at the railroad yards just outside of town.

Kyle didn't see what good looking at a railroad yard would do them, but he didn't raise any objections. Kale was already impatient with what he called Kyle's pickiness.

Kale sat there for quite a while, watching a couple of trains being made up. He nodded to himself as though he had made a great discovery. He grunted with satisfaction as he watched a car roll across the stretch of track and clang up against a string of cars.

"That's automatic coupling," he explained to Kyle. "I wonder how those cars are uncoupled."

"Hell, I don't know," Kyle replied. He was weary of this monotonous scene.

Despite Kyle's feeble protests, Kale spent the better part of two days hanging around the yards. "I know how they uncouple those cars," he announced triumphantly. "All they have to do is pull a pin."

That sounded simple enough, and Kyle said so. But what good would that piece of knowledge do?

"Sure, it's simple when the train isn't rolling," Kale answered. "It might be a little tougher, if the train's moving."

Kyle set his teeth. Kale got a lot of crazy ideas, and he might be getting another one. Kyle was only certain of one thing. He wasn't going to be the one to try and uncouple a car from a moving train. He had a vivid imagination, and he visualized slipping and falling between those cars. There wouldn't be enough left to interest a hungry dog.

Kale grinned maliciously at Kyle's expression. "You thinking of falling off, Kyle?"

"You're not picking *me* to do that job," Kyle yelped.

"God, you're blind," Kale said in disgust. "What do you think those rides out along the track the last couple of days meant?"

"I don't know," Kyle muttered.

"I don't know where you'd be if it wasn't for me," Kale said with contempt. Kale got a grip on his rising temper. "Didn't you notice that level piece of track some ten miles out of town?"

Kyle had seen that stretch, but it meant nothing to him. He shook his head.

"Oh, Jesus," Kale said bitterly. "What's beyond that long, level stretch? A long, steep grade. By the time a train reaches the top, it'll barely be crawling. A man could walk and almost keep up with it."

Kyle listened with renewed interest. "Go on," he said.

"We're after an express car," Kale said patiently. "That's where the money's usually carried. While the train is crawling up that grade, a man can step from his saddle in between the cars. He can pull the pin that couples them." His grin showed how pleased he was with himself. "The train goes on, and the uncoupled car rolls back down the grade. It'll stop somewhere along that level stretch."

"Not me," Kyle yelped. "I'm not going to step onto a moving train. Besides, how do you know that express car carries money? What if it isn't the last car on the train?"

Kale threw up his hands. "The damned, dumb questions you ask. Express cars always carry money. That's what they're made for. They're always the last car on the train. That's what I'm waiting for—to find the right train. I'm going to uncouple it. You can catch up my horse, can't you, and bring him back down the grade? Or is that too much to expect?"

Kale ignored the sarcasm. "Maybe you've got something," he admitted grudgingly.

"Maybe the train we're looking for will pull out to-morrow," Kale said. "All we do is wait and keep our eyes open."

On this basis, Kyle could go along with Kale. "I hope it's soon," he growled. "This waiting around is getting on my nerves."

"It'll happen soon," Kale assured him.

What Kale was waiting for happened the next day. His eyes glistened as he saw a work engine shunt an express car across a piece of track. Even from where they sat, Kyle and Kale could hear the clunk of the re-sultant bump. The express car was coupled to the wait-ing train.

Kale leaned over in his saddle. "This is what we've been waiting for. Let's go."

"They may put other cars on the train," Kyle ob-jected.

"No," Kale said impatiently. "That's already a long drag for an engine to pull up that grade. This is made to order."

Kyle shook his head. As the time for action grew closer, the less he liked it. "That train'll lose us in a few miles. It's almost ready to pull out now."

Kale looked at him in utter disgust. "I'm not planning on racing the train. We'll catch up with it when it hits that grade. We can cover some of the distance by leav-ing now."

Kyle kept looking back until Kale said, "Will you sit still? The train's coming. It'll pass us in a little while."

Kale was right. Kyle slewed around in his saddle when he heard the engine's whistle.

The train passed them, and the engineer blew the whistle again, leaned out of the cab window and gave them a friendly wave.

Kale returned the wave. "He doesn't know what's going to happen to his train," he said to Kyle and grinned. "I'd like to be around to see his face when he learns he lost his express car."

He demanded more speed from his mount, and Kyle followed suit. Kyle knew this wasn't going to work. Al-ready, the train had pulled far ahead. He started to say something about Kale being dead wrong, and Kale guessed his thoughts.

"That train will be easy to overtake," he said. "Wait and see."

Kyle was skeptical, but he didn't speak.

The grade started before Kyle was actually aware that it was beginning. He first noticed it in the laboring of the horses' strides. He looked ahead and couldn't believe his eyes. Even at the animal's slower speed, they were gaining on the train.

Kale grinned. "Maybe if you stay around me long enough, you'll learn something. I knew this grade would pull the train down."

Kyle ducked his head to hide his resentment. Kale always crowed whenever he was right. But maybe Kale had a right to feel cocky this time. The train was even slower than a walking horse. Kale and Kyle caught up with it before it was halfway up the grade.

The laboring engine made so much noise that it was difficult to talk over the sound. Kale whistled to catch Kyle's attention. He mouthed his words slowly, and while Kyle couldn't hear the words, he could understand what Kale was trying to say. Kale was going to make his attempt now. Kyle was to get ready to catch up Kale's horse.

Kyle's heart was in his throat as he watched Kale inch his horse nearer and nearer to the head of the express car. He spurred the horse for an additional burst of speed, then he was alongside the car. He reached out and caught the rungs of the ladder attached to the express car, kicked out of the saddle, and swung free. His feet scrambled for a foothold on the ladder.

He made it, lifted one hand, and waved to Kyle. Then he disappeared between the two cars. Kyle's heart resumed its normal beat. He whipped his horse to overtake the one Kale abandoned. He was too involved in catching Kale's horse to watch Kale unhook the car.

Kyle caught the horse, grabbed its reins, and turned back before he looked for Kale. The train was chugging steadily on, and for an instant Kyle thought Kale had failed. Then he saw the express car start rolling backward, picking up speed with every turn of its wheels.

Kale stood on the far end of the train. He dropped to the track and ran several steps to retain his balance. He didn't fall.

Kyle led Kale's horse to him, his eyes fixed on the ever increasing speed of the express car as it rolled back down the grade.

His eyes were admiring as he asked, "Was it hard, Kale?"

"It went just like I told you. Nothing to it. I pulled out that pin, and the car was free." He looked at the moving car and said, "We'd better be after it. We've got a lot of work to do."

Kyle thought the difficult part of the job was over. Here Kale was sounding as though new obstacles littered their path.

"What kind of work, Kale?"

Kale shrugged. "I don't know for sure until I look it over. First, we've got to get inside that car."

"I was thinking the car could jump the tracks and crash. Somebody could get killed."

Kale swore at him. "Go on. Keep worrying. Everything's gone smooth up to now, hasn't it?"

"We didn't set out to kill anybody," Kyle said stubbornly.

"And we're not going to," Kale snapped. "The track runs straight here. There's no curves to whip off a loose car. Come on. Let's get after it."

Kyle expected Kale to tear out at breakneck speed, but evidently Kale didn't think there was any hurry. It was a good thing, Kyle thought. These horses are pretty well spent. They'd better save what was left in them. They might need it later.

Kyle kept watching the runaway car. It seemed it would never slow down; then even his unpracticed eye could see that it was losing speed.

"Hah," Kale said in satisfaction. "Its momentum is running out. Didn't I tell you it would work out this way?"

There was that damned crowing again, but Kyle nodded. He couldn't argue against success. "You did, Kale," he said meekly. He thought of something, and

58

his face stiffened. "What if there is somebody in that car, and they put up a fight?"

"Oh, my God," Kale groaned. "There you go again. If you can't actually find trouble, you invent it."

Kyle's eyes smoldered. He was only pointing out what could happen. "Damn it, Kale—"

"Just shut up," Kale snapped.

They didn't exchange a word the remaining distance to the car. It looked lonely and abandoned as they approached it.

Kale rode up to the sliding door in the side and tried to move it. It wouldn't budge.

"Somebody's got it locked from the inside," he said. He raised his voice. "Hey, whoever you are, you better open up, if you know what's good for you."

"You go to hell," a voice replied. By the sound of the voice, Kale guessed the man inside was old. "What do you want?" the voice asked.

Kyle felt braver now and yelled, "You're all alone, old man. We cut your car loose. You're sitting out here all by yourself."

"Kinda figured that," the voice said, "from the way the car rocked going downgrade. Thought you'd be along soon."

"Open this door," Kale yelled.

He ducked wildly as a bullet tore through the door. The report was followed by a cackle. "Kinda looks like a standoff, don't it? You can't come in, and I can't get out."

Kyle had never seen greater rage seize Kale.

"You better use your head," Kale roared. "I brought dynamite with me. I'll blow up the whole damned car. You with it."

There was a long silence. Kale was ready to yell another warning when the voice came again. "Looks like you had everything figured out. I'm coming out, mister."

"Throw out that gun first," Kale ordered.

The door was cautiously eased back a crack, and a pistol was thrown out.

"I'm coming out, mister," the old man said. A thin,

59

sunken-chested old man appeared in the door. He grunted as he dropped to the ground.

"Young ones, ain't you?" the old man asked. "Just the two of you?" He seemed surprised that only two men would even attempt to stop and rob a train. "Won't do you any good. You'll be run down and caught, or shot. It's bound to happen."

"Keep your damned mouth shut," Kale raged. He clambered into the car and disappeared for a moment. He reappeared and said, "The damned safe is locked."

"Sure it is," the old man said complacently.

"Open it." Kale jabbed his pistol toward the old man.

"Can't," the old man replied. "I don't know the combination." He grinned, displaying gaps in his teeth. "Go ahead and shoot me, mister. It won't get you anyplace."

Kyle was afraid, from the rage seizing Kale's face, that he would do just that.

Kale made an effort and regained control of himself. "I wasn't lying when I said I brought dynamite with me just for something like this."

The old man looked uneasy. "Won't do you any good," he muttered.

"We'll see," Kale said grimly. He reached into his saddlebag and pulled out a wrapped bundle. "Watch this," he said. He hoisted himself back into the car and was out of sight for what seemed like an inordinately long time to Kyle.

"She's set and lit," Kale announced when he reappeared. "Better get back. I left a pretty long fuse, but I don't know how far the blast will reach."

Kale and Kyle herded the old man a good hundred yards from the car. Kale threw himself down behind a boulder. "You two better get down," he advised.

Oh God, Kyle thought in a frenzy. This was taking so long. At any moment, somebody could come by, and Kale's plan would be blown full of holes. It'd be smart to leave right now, but he kept his thoughts to himself. He took cover behind an adjoining boulder.

The growing tension was actually making Kyle's muscles ache. That damned dynamite was never going off. He started to question the delay when the blast came. It was deafening, slamming against his eardrums and making his head ring. Kyle thought he even felt a shock run through the ground.

Kale stood, and he was grinning broadly. "Thought I was lying, didn't you, old man? If you'd been hard-headed enough, you could have been in there."

Kyle was awed as he looked at the car. It was thoroughly wrecked, only the floor and wheels had any semblance to their original appearance. The dynamite had completely shattered the car. The roof was just a skeleton, and only a couple of supporting beams remained in place. The safe was blown onto its side, its door hanging askew.

"Jesus," the old man whispered as he looked at the ruin. He shook himself as though he visualized a frail human form being caught in that blast. "Beginner, ain't you? You used too many sticks."

Kale realized that, for his face turned a fiery red. "I got it open, didn't I?" he retorted savagely.

The three of them approached the shattered car. Kale stopped and stared at the ground. Bits of green paper literally covered the ground before them.

Kale's face was a study in bewilderment. "What the hell," he faltered.

The old man realized what those green pieces of paper were before Kale did. He cackled in obscene mirth and slapped his thigh. "Thought you were so damned smart, didn't you?" he choked out between cackles of laughter. "You blew the hell out of the safe all right. Don't you know what you're looking at, misters? Pieces of paper money. There was thirty thousand dollars in that safe, and you blew it all over the country." He went into another paroxysm of mirth.

Kale turned alternately red and white. His eyes bulged, and his throat was tight. The old man's insane cackling got on his nerves, and he shouted, "Shut up, damn you. You hear me? Shut up."

The old man stopped laughing and wiped a horny thumb across his eyes. "Didn't do you a damned bit of good, did it? And I can describe you. I'll never forget your faces."

"You won't remember them for long," Kale said in a frozen voice.

61

The old man stared at Kale, his face horror-stricken. "I didn't mean what I said," he managed to get out. "I won't say a word."

Kale's pistol was in his hand. "You're right there," he agreed.

Kale pulled the trigger, and the bullet hit the old man in the chest, slamming him backward. He hung there a long moment, accusation stamping his face. "No need to do that," he whispered.

Kale's frustration made him furious. "I told you to shut up." He pulled the trigger again and again.

The old man fell in a lifeless heap.

Kale was ready to shoot again, and Kyle stopped him. "Ain't no use," he said, stunned. "You already killed him. You really tore it wide open, Kale."

Kale lowered his pistol. He glared at the motionless figure and sought for words to justify himself. "I told him to shut up. He wouldn't listen."

Kyle kept shaking his head. "You killed him. You killed an old man." He was shaking inwardly, and it was beginning to show in his trembling lips. "They'll run us down now for sure."

"What else could I do?" Kale pleaded. "You heard him. He said he would describe us. I didn't think it was necessary to put the masks back on. Maybe I should have."

Kale was beginning to babble, and Kyle knew his confidence was shaken. "Don't make any difference now," he said in a beaten voice. "We'd better just get the hell out of here."

"He said there was thirty thousand dollars in that safe," Kale said in a broken voice. "My God! Thirty thousand dollars. It would have set us up for life." He reached down and scooped up a few bits of the green paper. "All that money gone," he mourned.

"Won't do any good to stand here and cry over it," Kyle said wearily. Kale was grieving over the lost money. He'd better start grieving over his hide.

The breeze stirred the bits of paper, and several of them danced in the air. Kale caught sight of a large piece and scrambled after it.

He came back with it in his hand, his eyes glowing.

"Look at this. A twenty-dollar bill with only a corner blown off. I'll bet it's still good."

Kyle shook his head in denial. With the old man's sightless eyes staring skyward, he didn't want to go around gathering up pieces of money. Every piece he picked up would only remind him of the shock and hurt on that old face when Kale shot him.

He looked uneasily about the horizon. He didn't see anything alarming, but just the same, he felt deep in his bones they'd better get out of here. If they were caught, the best they could hope for was a long jail sentence. At the worst, it would be a hanging. Kyle could imagine the public wrath over the wanton shooting of an old man. He licked his lips. "Kale, we'd better make tracks out of here while we still have the chance."

Kale was too busy running down more pieces of the money. Most of the fragments he threw away as being completely useless, but every now and then, he shouted with glee: "Another bill. Damn it, Kyle. Start looking. We've come this far. It'd be a crime not to pick up what good bills we can find."

Kyle gave in weakly. Maybe Kale was making sense. They should be able to get something out of this.

The pair searched for the better part of an hour. The search wasn't completely unrewarding. Both of them had bills stuffed in their pockets. Kyle was caught up in the thrill of the search. That hangdog look was gone from his face, and each new discovery increased that thrill.

"I guess that's all we can find," Kale finally said. "We got something out of it, boy. Let's see how much we have."

That pitiful body still lay over there. Kyle couldn't stand to stay around here any longer.

"No," he said firmly. "We'd better get out of here while we can."

"You could be right," Kale conceded reluctantly. "We'll count it later."

They put several miles between them and the body before they stopped and counted the money. They emptied their pockets into a pile, and Kale's elation grew as the total mounted.

"Over six hundred dollars," he said in a shaking voice. "And you had doubts all along. This beats the hell out of that stagecoach robbery, doesn't it?"

"We're not out of this yet," Kyle replied grimly. He had the unshakable instinct that they weren't out of it by a long way.

Chapter Ten

Verl came around the corner of the house and stopped short at the sight of Sam Travis. He almost pulled back, but it was too late. Travis had already seen him.

Verl sighed and moved forward toward Travis. He didn't particularly want to talk to him again. Coming so quickly on the heels of his other visit, Verl could bet this was no friendly visit either. He composed his face and said, "Howdy, Sam. What brings you out here so soon?"

Travis looked older and grayer, and Verl could swear his shoulders were more stooped. "Wish I could tell you this is just a friendly visit," Travis said gruffly. "But I can't."

"About Kale and Kyle again?" Verl asked. He couldn't quite keep the hostility out of his voice. Ever since Travis' last visit, Verl had been resentful of Travis' implications. Travis was damned quick to hang something on the twins when he had absolutely no proof. If Travis voiced more wild speculations, Verl didn't intend to handle him as gently this time.

"Better come in the house, Sam," he said quietly. "If it's about the twins, Jabez will want to hear it."

He let Travis precede him and followed him into the kitchen. "Pa, look who's here." Verl didn't mean for that jeering note to be so apparent in his tone.

Jabez looked stolidly at Travis. "What's he want this time, Verl?" The hostility was naked in his voice.

"Come on, Pa," Verl said sharply. "We've been friends for too many years to fall out now. Sam's only doing his job."

Jabez looked sheepishly at Travis. "Forget that, Sam. But you put some worry in my mind about my boys. Sit down. Coffee?"

"I'd appreciate that," Travis replied.

"Owen," Jabez called. "Pour Sam a cup of coffee."

This visit wasn't making Travis happy. He sat on the edge of his chair, twisting his hat around in his hand. Besides looking tired, he looked thoroughly miserable.

Owen set a cup of coffee before Travis.

"You might as well quit stewing and spit out what's choking you," Jabez said. "It'll be easier on all of us."

Travis still sought for a way to break his news. He knew Jabez's wrath when he was upset, and he didn't want to arouse it.

To avoid answering Jabez directly, Travis looked at Verl. "Did you ever talk to Dawson?"

Verl felt his face heat, and he felt a little guilty because he hadn't seen Dawson. Damn it, he thought angrily, I haven't committed any crime.

"No, I didn't, Sam," he confessed. "Things piled up here on the ranch, and they kept me hopping every minute. Without Kale and Kyle we're shorthanded. I kept planning on going in, and something always came up to make me put off the trip. Why?" he challenged.

"I wish you'd gone," Travis replied and sighed. "I don't think it would have done any good, but there was always the chance it might have. Dawson might have decided it would be wiser to talk to you."

Verl felt his neck cords stiffening. "You beating around the bush to announce more trouble, Sam?"

Travis shook his head, and there was genuine regret on his face. "I'm afraid so," he said miserably. "This time it's real bad trouble."

"Jabez told you to spit it out," Verl said harshly. "You're going to say it sooner or later. You might as well do it now."

Travis winced. "I guess you're right. Verl, a Union

Pacific train was held up just outside of Wilcox. The holdup men cut the express car loose on a steep grade. Let it roll back down until it came to a stop, then dynamited the safe. Blew the car all to hell. On top of that, they killed Charley Sims. He was the messenger in the express car. I fished with Charley several times. I talked to him less than a month ago. He told me he was going to retire this summer. Charley was a likable sort. Damned rotten shame. He worked forty-three years of his life and never got to enjoy his few remaining years. Those bastards gunned him down. Put three holes in him. Charley wasn't a violent man. I can't possibly believe he gave those two any reason to shoot him." He looked at three sagging jaws in shocked faces. "I saw Charley's body and the wrecked car. Don't try to tell me it didn't happen."

Jabez sounded as though he was choking as he tried to speak. "You came here to accuse the twins."

Travis looked squarely at him. "I'm not accusing anybody yet. But I damned sure want to ask them some questions. I want to find out where they've been spending their time. The further I look into this, the more signs I find. And they all point one way."

Jabez was ready to explode. Verl shook his head at him. "You got something else to go on?" he asked.

"A pair of men who looked alike were seen in Wilcox a couple of days before the train was jumped. The engineer who drove that train passed a couple of riders on the road the same day of the holdup. He remembers them well. Lonely country through there, and he doesn't see very many people. He waved to the riders, and they waved in return."

Verl stared at him. If Travis had an eyewitness, somebody who could definitely identify the twins as being on the spot at the right time, it would be damned hard evidence to tear down.

"And he can identify them, Sam?"

Travis shook his head. "He wasn't that close. He only knew they appeared to be of the same build, same height."

Verl snorted in derision. "Then, you admit you're only guessing. What the hell are you trying to pull,

Sam? Kale and Kyle are convenient targets. If you can pin this on them, it'll save you a lot of work."

Travis jumped to his feet, his face flaming. "Don't you go accusing me of trying to pin a crime on an innocent man. I never worked that way in my life."

Verl stood his ground. "This is beginning to look like it, isn't it, Sam? You need somebody to point at and say, They did it. Kale and Kyle are conveniently near."

"That's just it," Travis shouted. "They ain't near. All I'm trying to find out is where they are. What they've been doing." Hostility between the four men was thick enough to cut with a knife. "Look at it, Verl, from my viewpoint. How would it look to you, if you had the same facts?"

"No facts," Verl said obstinately. "You haven't proved a damned thing yet."

Stubbornness hardened Travis' face. "You've got to admit it's beginning to look damned suspicious. First, the stagecoach holdup, then the train. It looks like a couple of kids are beginning to work their way up the ladder." He pointed an accusing finger at Verl. "Damned funny you haven't tried to pin Dawson down. That's all I've got to say."

Verl was furious. "You've said enough. You've set your stubborn mind on the twins. You're not going to stop until you nail them."

He breathed hard to check himself from saying something that he might regret later. "All right, Sam. I'll see Dawson in the morning. I'll find out, one way or another, if he sold a gun to the twins. Does that suit you?"

Travis stood, and the weariness had returned, making him look more beaten than ever. "It'll help," he admitted grudgingly. "At least I might have a starting point. Damn it"—he looked appealingly at Jabez—"I want to clear this up as much as you do."

Jabez's face was stony hard. "I don't know," he muttered. "I just don't know."

Travis walked to the door. He stopped there and looked back. "I'll keep in touch with you."

"I imagine you will," Verl said sarcastically.

None of the Wakemans talked for a few moments after Travis left. Jabez seemed to have aged ten years in the short time it took for Travis to say what he had on his mind.

He looked so gray, so tired as he appealed to Verl. "Verl, what do you think?"

"I don't know," Verl said angrily. "But I can see it Travis' way. Two kids leave home, and right after that two holdups take place. Pa, you can't blame Travis for being suspicious."

"My God," Jabez said heavily. "I just can't believe Kale and Kyle would take this road."

"You don't know what to believe about them," Verl pointed out. "None of us ever knew what the twins were thinking."

Jabez briefly closed his eyes. "What are we going to do about this, Verl? If Travis is suspicious, it won't be long before that suspicion spreads. I think we'd better clear this up before it gets worse. Those damned fool twins." He was broodingly silent before he asked, "Are you going to see Dawson, like you told Sam?"

"You can rest easy on that," Verl assured him. He looked toward Owen. "Want to ride in to South Pass City with me in the morning?"

Eagerness touched Owen's eyes. Going into South Pass would give him another chance to see Etta. "I'm with you," he said promptly.

Chapter Eleven

"Kale, do you think it's wise to go back to South Pass City?" Kyle asked uneasily. They had money in their pocket. He was hoping Kale would be content to get out of this country.

"It fits with the plans I have," Kale answered absently. Right now, he had no worry of being tracked down. They had left no tracks, but it didn't eliminate his concern for the future. Two men were so vulnerable. He was going to ask Cassidy if he and Kyle could join the Wild Bunch. There would be comparative safety in numbers, and it would cool off any enthusiasm of the law to go after the Wild Bunch.

They rode quite a way in silence. "What are those plans?" Kyle ventured.

"You'll see."

It was an unsatisfying answer, but Kyle could see that Kale didn't intend to volunteer any information.

They pulled up before the poorest hotel in South Pass, and Kale said, "Go in and rent a room for us. I'll join you later." He untied the salesman's sample case from behind the saddle and handed it to Kyle.

Kyle looked at it with distaste. "What are we doing carrying that damned thing around with us? What good is it doing us?"

Kale winked at him. "It fits in with my plans, Kyle. You just take good care of it until I return."

Kyle swung down and, carrying the case, walked to the hotel door. He looked back at Kale and sighed. Kale was always so damned positive. Kyle had to admit things had turned out all right so far, but they'd had a lot of luck with them. Kale couldn't see the luck or admit it. Kyle turned and walked into the lobby. This beat-up old hotel would be glad to get paying guests of any kind. He wouldn't have any trouble renting a room here. He just wished everything ahead of them would go along as smoothly.

Kale made a thorough search of the town, looking for Butch Cassidy. He looked in saloons, restaurants, and pool halls. He didn't find Cassidy anywhere, and no one could tell him where Cassidy was. Kale was beginning to believe Cassidy had left town. Just thinking about it made him uneasy. The winter was over, and Cassidy usually stirred around in the spring.

Kale muttered an oath and kicked an inoffensive tin can, sending it clattering down the street. He had to talk to Cassidy; he had to convince him that Kale and Kyle could be valuable members in his bunch.

Just when he was beginning to despair of finding Cassidy, he saw him coming out of a barber shop.

Kale hurried to catch up with him. "Howdy, Mr. Cassidy," he said breathlessly. "Been looking all over for you. Do you remember me? You bought drinks for me and my brother a little while back."

"Sure, I remember you two," Cassidy replied. "The twins. Your brother all right?"

"He's fine," Kale said, a note of impatience in his voice. He wanted to get to the heart of the matter that was troubling him. "I'd like to talk to you."

Cassidy looked quizzically at him. "Something important?"

"It is to me," Kale replied. "Could we talk someplace in private?"

"I'm just going back to my hotel room. Kid Curry was there when I left. You want a place more private?"

"Your room will do just fine," Kale assured him.

"Good," Cassidy said briskly. If he was wondering what this was all about, nothing showed on his face.

Cassidy opened the door to his room, and Kid Curry lounged on Cassidy's bed.

"Damn it, Kid," Cassidy burst out. "Get your dirty boots off my bed. I've told you about that before."

Kid Curry grinned and swung his boots to the floor. "You always were picky." He looked curiously at Kale. "Who have we got here?"

"Kale Wakeman," Cassidy replied. "You met him and his brother. We bought them some drinks one afternoon."

Curry nodded in remembrance. "Sure, he had his twin brother with him. Can't forget that pair. You come back, kid, hoping for some more free drinks?"

Kale's face heated with indignation. Curry might think of him as a kid. He wouldn't after he listened to Kale's story.

"I've got something far more important on my mind," Kale growled. "Me and my brother would like to join your bunch."

Curry stared in amazement for a moment, then laughed with uproarious delight. He managed to get his

70

laughter under control and gasped, "Can you imagine that, Butch? Two snot-nosed kids think they can just walk up to us and join." He grinned tantalizingly at Kale. "I imagine quite a few men would like to join us. Hell, kid, we're not going around soliciting greenhorns. We're in a deadly serious business. One wrong move can get you a bullet right between the eyes. We're not trusting our lives to some fool kids. They make a mistake, and we pay for it."

Kale looked quickly at Cassidy. If Cassidy agreed with Curry, Kale was through, even before he got started.

"I'm sorry," Cassidy said gently. "What Curry said is right. Wait until you get a little older, then see me."

Kale choked back his rising anger. He knew what Cassidy was saying. In effect, he was saying, Grow up.

"Goddamn it," Kale shouted. He had their attention now, and he glared from face to face. "Kyle and me ain't no damned greenhorns. We've got a stagecoach robbery to our credit."

Cassidy's interest showed in his eyes. "Where did this so-called robbery take place?"

"Near Rawlins," Kale snapped. "Just Kyle and me pulled it off. Pulled it off clean."

"How much did you get out of it?" Curry asked.

"A hundred and ninety-four dollars." Kale couldn't keep the bragging note out of his voice.

"Christ!" Curry exclaimed. "You expect to impress us with that?" He spit on the floor. "Hell, that ain't enough to even saddle up a horse for."

Kale looked mutely at Cassidy, hoping that Cassidy didn't downgrade that robbery as Curry did.

"I heard something about that robbery," Cassidy mused. "So it was you two who pulled it off." He tried to keep his face straight, but a grin twitched at his lip corners. "Wasn't much of a haul, was it? Didn't you do any planning? Did you try to find out what the stagecoach might be carrying?"

Kale felt the heat of embarrassment steal into his face. "I guess not," he muttered. "We just took the first stage that came along."

Curry started to spit on the floor again, and Cassidy

roared: "You do that again, and I'll throw your ass out of here. No wonder people call you The Tramp."

Curry wasn't abashed. "Picky," he said again. He went back to tormenting Kale. "I told you he was nothing but a greenhorn."

Kale was pushed beyond his endurance. "Greenhorn?" he yelled. "How about that train robbery outside of Wilcox. Do you think that was pulled off by greenhorns?"

Cassidy showed more interest. "Did you two pull that too? Ease off him, Kid," he ordered Curry. "I want to hear more about this. Go on, Kale. Tell me about it."

"We caught the train on a steep grade. I swung onto it and uncoupled the express car. It rolled back down the grade and came to a stop on a level stretch."

"How did you get into that car?" Cassidy asked. "Didn't somebody put up some kind of a resistance?"

Kale was carried away by the renewed respect Cassidy was showing. "Sure, the old man did. But I told him I'd blow the damned car up around him if he didn't open that door. I carried dynamite in my saddlebag." He glared defiantly at Curry. "Tell me I didn't plan for that."

Even Curry showed more respect. "You used your head, kid," he admitted. "How much was the car carrying?"

Kale wanted desperately to impress him. "Thirty thousand dollars," he said slowly.

He couldn't believe his ears. Both Cassidy and Curry were laughing, laughing at him. "I heard about that train robbery too," Cassidy said. "You blew that thirty thousand dollars all to hell."

Kale was sick to his stomach. He hung his head and wouldn't look at Cassidy. "I used too much dynamite," he mumbled. "But we picked up some good bills, over six hundred dollars." Maybe that would restore some of his shattered standing.

Cassidy and Curry were roaring with laughter now, and Kale stood. He couldn't take much more. "I guess I'd better go now," he said with as much dignity as he could muster.

"Sit down," Cassidy ordered. "You did pretty good.

One little thing went wrong." His lips twitched again, but he didn't break out into that dignity-stripping laughter. "Could've happened to anybody."

He looked at Curry. "What do you think?"

"For kids, they did pretty good," Curry conceded. "But they're still pretty green. Do you want to nursemaid them right now?"

Cassidy gave the question serious consideration, then decided against it. "Not right now," he finally said.

He stood and crossed the room to where Kale sat and placed a friendly hand on his shoulder. "I'll keep you in mind, Kale. Maybe in the fall we can get together. If they don't pick you up before then."

Kale felt his eyes sting. He wanted to rant and rave. He had been so damned close.

Cassidy saw his misery, and his face softened. "I'll tell you this, kid. You get in a bad jam and need help and I'm around, you let me know. I might be able to help you out."

Kale defiantly threw back his head. He didn't need Cassidy to get along. He could make out all right on his own.

"Sure," he said flatly and stalked to the door, his boot heels resounding against the floor.

Chapter Twelve

"I don't give a damn what happens to the twins," Verl said fiercely as he and Owen rode toward South Pass City. "But they're tearing the guts out of Pa. I heard him limping around in his room all night. I would gladly break their necks for causing him that misery."

Owen nodded grave agreement. "I guess a parent

never gets beyond the hurt their kids can cause them. Do you think the twins pulled that train holdup, Verl?"

"Hell, no," Verl exploded. "I don't know about the stage robbery, but they didn't have a hand in holding up the train. You heard Travis say two men blew up the express car. Where would they learn to use dynamite? No way. That's why I came down on Sam so hard. I just can't tie them and dynamite together."

He started to add something, and his jaw dropped.

Owen, watching him, asked, "What is it, Verl?"

"Do you remember when Pa and I blasted out those rocks to open up the creek so it could run into that bottom hayfield? Kale was with us all the time. He went into town with me when I bought that dynamite, and he asked a million questions when Pa used it. I've never seen anybody so fascinated with explosives." A sigh broke his long silence. "I guess I jumped on Sam too fast and too hard. Kale has a quick and inquisitive mind. When he learned something, he retained it."

Owen stared at him amazed. "You changing your thinking now?"

"I'm changing it enough to say it's possible they could be involved."

Owen decisively shook his head. "Naw," he disclaimed. "A kid wouldn't remember that dynamite. Damn it, that was years ago, Verl."

Verl's face was heavy with thought. "That's the trouble, Owen. No one ever knew what was going on in Kale's mind, and where Kale went, Kyle followed. I'm just saying the possibility definitely exists." He stared unseeingly ahead of him. "Sure, Kyle would do whatever Kale told him. If Kale wanted to make a big splash, holding up a train would do it." He shook his head. "He was certainly smarting when he left home. Maybe he saw a way to make all of us sorry."

"What are you going to do, Verl? Tell Travis about the dynamite?"

"No," Verl said flatly. "The twins are still family. Do you think I want to point that old, tired bird dog in a definite direction because I've got some suspicions? No, I'll have to see far more solid proof than I can see now."

Owen stared straight ahead. "Poor Pa," he said softly. "Do you think he fears the same thing you do, Verl?"

Verl shrugged. "Who knows? But I think a father has instincts where his sons are concerned." He silently echoed Owen's words: "Poor Pa." Jabez was going through a certain hell right now.

Neither of them spoke again the remainder of the way to South Pass.

Verl pulled up before Creed Dawson's shop. "No need for you to stay around, Owen. It might be better if I went in alone. Both of us might make Dawson think he was being ganged up on. It could make him clam up more than ever."

Owen's eagerness shone in his eyes. "I might as well go on over and see Etta while you finish your business here."

Verl grinned. That was what Owen wanted all the time. "Go ahead. I'll pick you up there."

He watched Owen ride down the street. At least Kale's leaving home had erased one problem for Owen. Owen wouldn't be bothered by Kale slipping into town to see Etta.

He turned toward the door. He just wished every problem could be solved so easily.

He stepped into the shop, his face blank. Dawson saw him coming, and his agate eyes were on Verl every step he took.

"Anything I can do for you, mister?" Dawson asked. Verl's unwavering stare was making him nervous, for tiny beads of sweat broke out on his forehead.

"You know who I am," Verl snapped. "I'm Verl Wakeman."

Dawson nodded reluctantly. "I thought you was."

"And you know my two brothers, Kale and Kyle."

Dawson pondered over that a moment, then shook his head. "I might have seen them, but I don't know them."

"You should know them," Verl announced. "You sold them a gun."

That made Dawson swallow hard. Verl was sure he saw Dawson's Adam's apple run up and down in his

75

throat, and that could be an uneasy flicker in his eyes.

Dawson's face turned raw and violent. "You're out of your mind. I never did any business with those boys at any time." His belligerence grew with each passing moment. "What's it to you? I don't see you wearing a badge."

Verl regarded him speculatively. It was a known fact that Dawson did business with many of the outlaws. Lawmen had tried to make him talk about his transactions with them, but with no success. Verl doubted he would have any better luck, but he had to try.

His hands snaked out over the counter and clamped about Dawson's throat. Verl put enough pressure in his thumbs to put a darkening in Dawson's face, and his breathing sounded labored.

Dawson tried to pry Verl's hands from his throat, but he wasn't strong enough. His fists flailed futilely at Verl's wrists. "You've gone plumb out of your mind," he gasped.

"They're my brothers," Verl said. "Talk, or I can choke an answer out of you."

"If you do, you'll be the sorriest man who ever lived," Dawson wheezed.

Verl saw that this tack wasn't going to win. He could beat Dawson to a pulp, but he wouldn't talk. He shoved Dawson away in disgust. He put enough force into the move to send Dawson reeling several feet before he slammed against a wall. Dawson fought to keep his feet, flailing his arms. He managed to retain his balance and hung there against the wall, gasping for breath. He tried to speak, and for a moment he could only splutter.

Verl leveled a finger at him. "All right, Dawson." The words were admission of temporary defeat. "You won't tell me what I want to know. But your time around here's running short. One of these days, decent people will be sickened of your kind. If they don't hang you, you'll be run out of town."

"Big talk," Dawson sneered.

Verl stared at him, then shook his head, turned, and walked to the door. He expected Dawson to say something before he opened the door, but Dawson wisely decided not to push Verl any farther.

Verl stepped through the door and slammed it behind him. He stood in sober reflection before he moved to his horse. He felt that Dawson had sold a gun to Kale, for he sensed an admission in him. Some great fear held Dawson's tongue. Once it was known that he talked freely of his dealings, every outlaw would turn against him. The fear of that was greater than any fear of Verl manhandling him.

Verl mounted and turned his horse toward Etta's house. He hoped Owen had a more enjoyable time than he had with Dawson. Damn you, Kale, he muttered. You stirred up a real mess this time. I hope it pleases you.

Chapter Thirteen

Kale walked into the shabby hotel. He was shaken by anger and frustration. If only he could have hooked up with Cassidy, all his worries would be over. He had been so damned close; he knew it. For a moment, Cassidy had considered his request before he turned him down.

To hell with him, Kale thought spitefully. We don't need his damned bunch.

He walked through the rundown lobby, where an old man dozed behind the desk. Kale reached over and rudely shook him awake. "My brother came in a little while ago. Which room did he take?"

The old man blinked bleary eyes at Kale, then they cleared. "Sure, I remember him. He looks just like you. He's in Room 105." This was a tough-looking man before him, and he was eager to please him. "Anything else I can do for you?"

Kale kept walking. He didn't even turn his head at

the question. The old man muttered and went back to his interrupted nap.

Kale didn't bother to knock on 105. As rundown as this hotel was, he doubted there was a lock in the place that worked.

His unexpected entrance startled Kyle, and he squeaked. He looked at Kale, and a flush of mortification spread across his face. "Don't you ever knock?"

Kale grinned bleakly. "Any reason I should?" A bad case of nerves was riding Kyle. That furtive, harried look had grown on his face with each passing day.

It wasn't any use getting sore at Kale, for it didn't bother him one way or the other. Kyle swallowed hard and said weakly: "You weren't gone very long. Was your trip a success?"

"No," Kale replied. "I talked to Cassidy about joining his bunch. He turned me down flat."

That harried look was more apparent on Kyle's face. He, too, realized what the feeling of security of belonging to the Wild Bunch would give them. "What are we going to do, Kale?" There was almost a whimper in his voice.

"We'll do just as we did before. Do without him. We got along all right without his help, didn't we?"

Kyle licked lips, which had suddenly gone dry. "I don't know, Kale. It ain't over yet. They may be looking for us."

"Christ," Kale yelped. "You starting that up again? Nobody's looking for us. They don't even know who they're looking for."

"But they might," Kyle insisted. "We don't know what's in their heads. I still say we'd better make tracks out of here."

"Not until I do what I came to South Pass for," Kale said stubbornly. He unsnapped the case and opened it. He took a half-dozen dresses out of the case and spread them out on the bed. "Which one do you think Etta would like best?"

"Oh God," Kyle moaned. "We're hanging around here just to give Etta a dress? It could cost us dear."

"Will you shut up!" Kale yelled. "I know what I'm doing."

"All right," Kyle said wearily. *"Your* way."

Kale nodded in satisfaction. "Help me pick out a dress."

Kyle liked the red one with the black stripes down the skirt. Kale nodded. He sorta leaned that way himself.

"Aren't you going to give her all of them?" Kyle asked.

Kale winked at him. "And run the risk of spoiling her? This one will do for now."

He packed the other dresses back in the case and snapped it shut. He carried the red dress over one arm and picked up the case. "Come on."

"Aren't we coming back here?" At Kale's shaking head, Kyle howled, "I paid for a night's lodging."

"What did it cost you, a couple of dollars?" Kale asked contemptuously. "So we lose it. Real important money."

Kyle grumbled about the waste of money all the way to the street. "We ain't got money to throw around, Kale."

"We'll get more," Kale said carelessly. "Now, will you quit harping on it?"

He retied the case onto the back of his saddle before he mounted.

Kyle didn't speak until they reached the Faber house. "What if old Cleatis is home?"

Kale frowned at him. "What if he is? It won't make any difference."

"He might not appreciate you giving one of his girls a dress."

Kale admitted that Kyle might have a point, and he thought about it before he answered. "I'll manage some way to see that Etta and I are alone." He scowled at his brother. "Does that satisfy you?"

"It helps."

Ann Faber answered Kale's knock. Kale had the dress folded up and tucked under his arm. Ann's eyes went to it, but she didn't ask any questions.

"Etta home?" Kale asked.

"She is," Ann said coolly. Her dislike was plain in her voice.

"Will you tell her I'm here?"

Ann nodded in resignation. "Wait in the parlor. I'll tell her."

"Is Cleatis home?" Kale asked.

"Why?" Her eyes flooded with suspicion.

"I just wanted to say hello to him."

The suspicion didn't fully fade, but Ann said: "He's gone next door to visit a neighbor. Do you want me to get him?"

Kale quickly shook his head. "No, it's not that important."

Ann left them in the parlor. Kale winked at Kyle. The wink said, Didn't I tell you everything would work out all right?

Etta came into the parlor, and her face was stiff and set.

"Ain't you glad to see me, Etta?" Kale asked.

"It took you long enough to come back," she said coldly. "Tell me why I should be glad."

"Important business held me up, Etta." Kale took the dress from under his arm and shook out the wrinkles. "I thought this might make you happy. Doesn't it prove I was thinking about you all the time?"

Etta's face was rapturous, and she squealed with joy. She seized the dress from Kale's hand and held it up before her. "Oh, it's just beautiful," she cooed. "And it looks like a perfect fit. And the colors. How did you know what I'd like?"

Kale grinned. "Just instinct, I guess. When I saw that dress, I told myself, That's for Etta."

"I've got to reward you for this," Etta cried.

"You don't see me backing up, do you?" Kale countered.

Etta flew at him, her arms outstretched. She wrapped them around his neck and kissed him. Maybe she intended it to be just a simple, grateful kiss, but it didn't turn out that way.

Kyle saw her arms tighten as she clung tightly to Kale. Their mouths didn't separate for several moments.

Ann picked the wrong time to enter the parlor. "What's going on here?" she demanded.

80

Etta wasn't in the least abashed. "I was just thanking Kale for this gift," she said and held out the dress.

Ann looked as though she couldn't believe her eyes. "That's shameless," she said heatedly. "What will Pa think if he knows you're taking gifts of clothing from a man?"

Etta tossed her head. "I don't care. This dress is mine, and I'm not going to give it up."

"You've lost your mind," Ann said, tight-lipped. "Wait until Pa talks to you. You'll do what he says. You still live here."

Etta's face flamed. "Maybe I've lived here too long."

"What does that mean?" Ann demanded.

Before Etta could answer, Ann heard a knock on the front door. "I'll see who it is." Ann pointed a finger at Etta. "This isn't over, young lady. We've got a lot more talking to do."

"It won't do any good," Etta shouted after her. "You've tried to boss me around for too long. I'm old enough to know what I want to do."

Ann's face sagged as she walked toward the door. Etta had always been difficult to handle. Now, all the rebellion in her nature was surfacing.

She opened the door, and her heart sank. This was the last person she wanted to see at this house right now.

Owen looked curiously at her. "Something bothering you, Ann? You look funny."

Ann mutely shook her head.

Owen's eyes searched her face again, then he asked, "Is Etta here?"

Ann had to have a reason to turn Owen away, and she searched frantically for the most plausible. "She's here, Owen. But she isn't feeling well. It'd be better if you came back some other time."

"Something's going on here," Owen said quietly. "I think I'd better talk to her right now. Where is she?"

Ann shook her head, and Owen growled, "All right, I'll find her." His eyes bored into her face. "You're trying to hide something, Ann," he accused.

She shook her head again and tried to compose her

face. "It's not that at all, Owen. If you'll give me just a moment to explain—"

"No," he said impatiently. He pushed by her and strode toward the parlor. He stopped short as he looked into it. He turned his head, and his expression reproached Ann. "I didn't think you'd do this," he said heavily.

"It's not what you think, Owen," she said desperately. "They came here uninvited." She caught his arm. "Let me talk to you somewhere else in the house. Then maybe you'll understand."

"The hell I will," Owen shouted. He threw off her hand and stepped into the room. His face was disbelieving as he looked at Etta, then at Kale and Kyle.

"I told you to stay away from here, Kale," Owen said huskily. "You should've paid attention. Maybe now it's too late."

Kale's face was wooden, but there was a mocking note in his voice as he asked, "What's that supposed to mean?"

"It means Travis is looking for you. He thinks you're involved in a train robbery."

Kyle shut his eyes and shuddered. The sound escaping his lips was half sob, half moan.

Owen put all his attention on Etta. "You didn't do him any favor in encouraging him." He noticed the dress she still held in her hands. "What's this?" His voice was ugly with suspicion.

Etta defiantly tossed her head. "Kale brought it to me." She flushed at the bitter accusation in Owen's eyes. "You don't own me. You can't tell me what I can or can't accept."

Owen tried to beat back his rage, but it rose in a surge he couldn't control. "I'll show you what I think about accepting gifts from him." He jerked the dress from her, and two powerful hands ripped it in half.

Etta screamed, and it was an enraged sound. Kale reacted to the same rage but more violently. He sprang toward Owen, his face working furiously.

"What the hell do you think you're doing?" he roared.

Owen had more than he could stand. He gladly met

Kale's charge. "You always learned things the hard way," he said grimly. "You'll remember this time."

He knocked Kale's swinging arm aside, half turning him. It left Kale's face in profile, and Owen swung at the exposed jaw. He put all the force he had in the blow. It landed on the hinge of Kale's jaw, and it should have knocked him out.

Kale fell hard, his head rapping against the floor. He lay there, blinking his dazed eyes, trying to put things back into clearer focus.

Owen stood over him, his face working with a savage eagerness. "Get up," he begged. "Or I'll kick you to pieces."

Kale's eyes cleared, and he stared at Owen with murderous rage. "I told you once before, nobody is going to hit me." He scrambled for the gun at his hip, and when it came out, it was pointed at Owen.

For the first time, Owen fully realized what he faced. He hadn't brought a gun into town with him, and Kale had completely lost his head. If he was going to stop Kale, it had to be with his fists or feet. He measured the distance between them with a calculating eye. One long stride would carry him to Kale. Then he could kick the gun out of his hand.

He bunched his muscles under him and sprang toward Kale.

Kale correctly read Owen's intentions, and he screamed, "I told you, but you wouldn't listen." He pulled the trigger, and the blast of the gun was ear-shattering in the small room.

The impact of the bullet flung Owen back a staggering step, and he fought to remain on his feet. "Why, you did it," he said in a wondering tone. "You did—"

"I told you," Kale screamed. He pulled the trigger again.

Owen's face set in cold shock. He tried to say something, but the words were garbled. Each effort to speak spewed blood across the room. He sank to the floor, an incredulous expression molding his face.

"You killed him," Kyle said in a shocked voice. "You killed Owen."

"What the hell did you expect me to do?" Kale snarled as he scrambled to his feet. "Should I have laid there and have him kick my head off?"

He looked at Etta. Her face was sagging into ruin, and her mouth was open. Another instant, and she would be screaming. He glanced at Ann. Shock still held her, but in another instant she would be screaming too.

"Kyle and I are going to get out of here," Kale said harshly. "You want to go with us or stay here?"

Etta was whimpering, almost like an animal in pain.

"Make up your mind," Kale snapped.

She glanced frantically at him, then at her sister. Everybody would blame her for her part in this. "I'm going with you," she sobbed.

Kale grabbed her arm. "Good! Let's get moving."

He started for the door, and Ann blocked his way. "You're not leaving," she said, determination hardening her face. "You're not running away."

Kale held Etta with one hand, the gun in the other. He swept out the arm holding the gun, and the barrel hit Ann sharply on the cheekbone. She tried to make a sound, but her eyes were glazing. She fell in a heap.

Etta whimpered again, and Kale's fingers bit more deeply into her arm. "She was trying to stop us," he said harshly. "Did you want that?"

She shook her head, and the whimpering was her only protest.

"Let's get going, then," Kale said and shoved her ahead of him. The three ran out the front door, and Kale didn't take time to close it.

"We'll take Owen's horse," Kale said. He helped Etta up into the saddle, then mounted his horse. The look on her face scared him, and he tried to erase it by saying: "Don't worry about that dress Owen destroyed. I've got more for you. Your worries are over. I'm going to take good care of you."

She looked at him, and some of the confusion cleared from her face. "Where are we going, Kale?"

"You leave that to me," he said cockily. He wasn't going to have any more trouble with Etta. He glanced over at Kyle. Kyle stared ahead, his features locked in a frozen trance. Kale was going to have far more trouble with Kyle. He shrugged off the irritation. Hadn't he always been able to handle Kyle?

Chapter Fourteen

Kale left Kyle and Etta in the lobby of the hotel where Cassidy stayed. Oh God, let Cassidy be in. But even more, let him listen.

He knocked on the door and tried to get the shakiness out of his body. God, it was so bad, his knees were even trembling. He just hoped it didn't show in his voice.

Cassidy opened the door and, beyond him, Kale saw Kid Curry still lounging on the bed. It looked as though Cassidy and Curry hadn't left the room.

"Did you forget something?" Cassidy asked.

Kale gulped, drew a deep breath, then said, "Mr. Cassidy, I'm in trouble, bad trouble."

Cassidy's keen eyes evaluated him, and a slight frown stamped his face at what he saw. Kale's face was pasty, and Cassidy could almost swear that Kale's voice was near the breaking point.

"You better come in and tell me all about it," he said matter-of-factly. He stepped aside for Kale to enter.

Cassidy sat down on the edge of the bed and waved Kale to a chair. "What's got you in such a sweat? It must've happened fast. You sure didn't look like this when you left here."

Kale locked his hands together to keep them from shaking. He kept his eyes on them. He had to have something to focus his attention on. Oh God. He was afraid he was going to break down.

"Didn't you hear Butch?" Curry asked impatiently. "He's waiting."

Kale's first attempt to speak came out as a rasping croak. He swallowed hard and said in a jerky voice, "I just killed my brother."

Curry sat bolt upright on the bed. He swore loudly.

Cassidy's expression didn't change. "You better tell me about it," he said slowly.

"We had an argument." Kale's voice faltered, then steadied. "He knocked me down. It's happened before. I warned him that nobody was ever going to hit me again. Things just sorta turned red. I drew and shot him."

Cassidy was absorbed in this story. "Was he armed?" he asked.

"No." Kale fought to keep his voice steady. "Damn it, he hit me." Despite his efforts, his voice kept rising. "I wasn't expected to take that, was I?" he asked wildly.

A long silence fell in the room. Curry broke it first. "I'll say one thing. You showed spunk. It proves you won't let anybody push you around, regardless of who he is." He reflectively stroked his chin with thumb and forefinger. "I've done the same thing. I like a man who keeps his word. If any man hit me, I'd blast a hole in him too."

Cassidy glanced at Curry and grimaced. "You would," he said flatly. "You always had a taste for blood." He looked back at Kale. "You came to me for some reason. What is it?"

"Let me ride with you," Kale pleaded. "I've got to get out of South Pass as fast as I can. Verl, my older brother, will be looking for me. When he hears about this, he'll go crazy. Verl and Owen were very close."

Cassidy grinned bleakly at him. "Makes things kinda sticky, don't it? What do you think, Curry?"

Curry's eyes were half-closed as he speculated on the problem Cassidy posed. "He did what he had to do. Right now he's in a bind. Hell, Butch, we've been in binds ourselves. And a lot of times, other people pulled us out. He might be a good man to have with us."

Kale lifted his head, and elation began to flood his

face. Curry was for him. That should swing Cassidy. The elation was dashed when he saw Cassidy's slowly shaking head.

"I don't know," Cassidy mused. "Might be pulling trouble down on us, trouble not of our own making."

Curry snorted. "Just when did *that* bother you?"

"I'd do whatever you told me," Kale begged.

Cassidy stared at him a moment, then he came to the decision that was so slow in forming. "We were just talking about leaving tonight. Spring's here. Time to get back to work." He glanced at Kale squint-eyed. "Maybe I'm getting foolish in my old age." He sighed and flung up his hands. "All right, you can ride with us. But the first time you get the inclination to go off on your own or argue with me about anything, I'll shoot you or kick your ass out."

"There's one other thing," Kale said shakily. "My brother's with me. He's downstairs in the lobby."

"Figured he would be," Cassidy said, a note of impatience in his voice.

Kale's head bobbed rapidly. "There's somebody else down there too. A woman."

"Oh, for God's sake!" Cassidy exploded.

Curry grinned all over his face. "That might be interesting, Butch." He tried to suppress his laughter as he looked at Kale. "Is she a looker?"

"She's my girl," Kale said heatedly. "I promised her I'd take care of her." He locked eyes with Curry.

Curry was beginning to bristle, and Cassidy broke up the threatening storm. "You know what Nettie would do to you if she caught you even looking at another woman."

Curry's tough expression relaxed. "Don't I?" he said hollowly and grimaced.

Cassidy studied Kale. He didn't like the thought of another woman being added to his bunch. He didn't know how she would get along with the other women, and he could sense impending trouble. This newcomer could be far more trouble than she was worth.

Kale sensed his unhappy thoughts and cried: "I promise she'll be no trouble. She can ride, and she can shoot. I taught her how. She could even be a help." He waited, almost holding his breath, for Cassidy's final decision.

"Well, all right," Cassidy finally said with reluctance. "I can tell you one thing you can bank on. If she becomes too much trouble, out she goes." He groaned, as though he was suddenly irritated. He felt as though this whole damned thing had been forced on him.

Kale was relieved. Everything had turned out better than he had hoped for.

"When do we leave?" he asked.

"Sometime tonight," Cassidy replied.

Kale's face fell, and Cassidy snapped, "Doesn't that suit you?"

"It isn't *that*," Kale said. Things were beginning to close in around him again. "I don't know what to do with the time between now and then. I can't stay around South Pass that long. When Verl finds out about Owen, he'll be looking for me."

Cassidy's grin had a frosty tinge. "Being in a bad bind isn't so pleasurable, is it? But I can fix that. Do you know where Frenchy Farquer's shack is? Just outside of town. Frenchy died six years ago. Nobody moved into his place."

Kale had to think for a moment before his face cleared. He was sure he knew which shack Cassidy meant. It was a rundown hovel, each year growing more weary- and abandoned-looking.

"I know where it is. Kyle and me looked into it several years back." He didn't want to tell Cassidy that they had played in the shack. That made him sound too youthful.

Cassidy nodded. "We'll pick you up there tonight. I don't know exactly when, but we'll be there."

Kale stood, filled with new confidence. Wait until he told Etta and Kyle about this new arrangement. It should wipe that hangdog look off their faces.

"We'll be waiting." He squared his shoulders and stalked out of the room.

"Doesn't take much to bring him back to life," Curry observed.

An absent grin touched Cassidy's lips. "He was one

88

scared kid when he thought he wasn't going to be accepted." His voice harshened. "I hope to God I haven't bought trouble."

Curry shrugged. "Quit stewing. Everything might turn out for the best. Hell, he could become one of the best men you ever had. I'll say one thing—he started out with a bang. Hell, Butch. Everybody has to start one way or another."

Cassidy's eyes were still worried. "I hope to God you're right."

Chapter Fifteen

Verl pulled up before the Faber house and frowned at the open front door. It wasn't warm enough yet to leave a door open this time of the year.

He dismounted and walked up on the porch. "Anybody home?" he called. Owen should be here, but his horse was nowhere in sight.

Verl didn't like this silent house. It gave him an eerie, clammy feeling that made his skin prickle.

He put more volume into his voice. "Hey! Anybody home?"

"I'm here," Verl heard Ann call. It didn't sound like her normal tone. She sounded subdued and shaken.

Verl heard low voices talking in the parlor before he reached it. He looked into the parlor, and his face went taut and white with shock. Ann sat on the floor, and Owen's head was in her lap. Ann had a cut on a cheekbone that still oozed blood. Owen wasn't moving at all. Verl's eyes fixed on the ghastly red stain on his shirt front.

Cleatis sat in a chair, his head drooping, his face heavy with stupefaction.

Verl barely glanced at him as he asked in a choking

voice, "How bad is he?" He knew the answer to that question even before it was answered.

Cleatis answered for Ann. "He's dead, Verl. I was next door and heard the shooting. I got over here as fast as I could. Ann was unconscious, and Owen wasn't moving. I saw I couldn't do anything for him. I put all my efforts to reviving Ann."

Ann closed her eyes, and a sob racked her body.

Verl didn't want her breaking down now; he had to know what had happened here.

"Who did it, Ann?" His eyes stung from unshed tears. That was Owen down there, and Verl would never talk to him again. For an agonizing moment the sense of loss was overpowering.

He knelt down beside Ann. "Ann, I've got to know. Who did it?"

She looked at him through tear-dimmed eyes. "Kale," she said in a barely audible voice. "I tried to stop him. He hit me with a gun barrel as he ran out." She closed her eyes again, and tears ran slowly down her cheeks.

Verl gripped her shoulder. She was reliving a horrible moment, but she couldn't stop now—not until she told him all she knew.

"Go on," he said fiercely.

She swallowed hard, then went on in a faint, reedy voice. "Owen and Kale were arguing over Etta. Kale had given her a dress. Owen objected to that. He knocked Kale down, and Kale went wild. He swore nobody could hit him and get away with it. He pulled his gun and aimed at Owen. Owen tried to stop him, but it was no use. Kale fired twice, and Owen fell."

Verl's face was a cold mask of hatred. His thoughts were chaotic, but he managed to say: "Owen wasn't armed. He didn't bring a gun with him."

Ann nodded mutely. The gesture said she knew.

Verl looked squarely at the dead face of his brother for the first time. There was agony stamped on it. Owen hadn't died easy.

Verl stood, and he was suddenly old, his legs almost refusing to support him. "Did Kale say where he was going, Ann?"

90

She looked up at him, and she was crying hard now. Her face was contorted, and tears ran down her cheeks. "I didn't hear, Verl," she gasped. "Kyle was with him."

Verl's eyes blazed as he looked at her. He could have expected that.

"Etta went with them," Ann said in a broken voice.

"Damn him," Cleatis broke out. "He took my daughter."

Verl barely glanced at Cleatis. He didn't give a damn what happened to Etta. He suspected she went willingly enough. Etta's going should be to Verl's advantage. A woman could only slow them down.

"Ann, will you take care of Owen," Verl asked in a lifeless voice, "until I get back?"

"Yes," she whispered. She looked as though she wanted to say something else.

Verl waited a moment, but no words came. He couldn't stay any longer. Every passing moment was to Kale's advantage.

"I'll be back, Ann." Verl turned and strode to the door.

Cleatis called after him, "You just bring Etta back."

Verl didn't even turn his head.

God, just climbing into the saddle seemed such a terrible effort. Verl briefly closed his eyes before he swung up. That tiny hesitation was his only visible display of emotion. Verl's crying was all inside, a terrible weeping that twisted and tore him.

Goddamn you, Kale, he thought, and his head cleared a little. He wasn't looking for his brother; he was looking for a murderer.

He had no idea which direction to turn, or where to begin his search. He turned his horse toward the main portion of South Pass City.

He had to have a starting point, and he pondered dully over it. He was filled with self-blame. In a way, he was responsible for Owen's death. If only he had listened to Travis and voiced his own suspicions about Kale, this could have been averted.

There was no use in this self-recrimination, but he persisted. He had handled everything wrong. He thought dully of getting no information from Dawson.

While he was engaged in that useless quest, Owen was alone and facing Kale. Verl's soul writhed in agony. He should have been with Owen. He could have prevented what had happened.

Dawson's name popped into his mind again. By God, Dawson should know any news about Kale. Dawson was well versed on the doings of the outlaws.

Verl pulled up before Dawson's shop. At least, it was a starting point. A moment ago, he didn't have that much.

He strode into the building, and Dawson looked fearfully at the savage face that confronted him. He didn't know what had happened, but it had to be bad to make Verl look like this.

"Where's Kale and Kyle?" Verl demanded in a rasping voice.

Dawson started to tremble, and his mouth went slack. He looked at a crazy man, a man in a killing rage.

Dawson licked dry lips. "I—I don't know what you mean," he stuttered.

Verl pulled out his gun and leveled it at Dawson. "Don't lie to me, you bastard. I'd just as soon blow off your head."

Dawson had to grip the edge of the counter to remain upright. If he ever looked at madness, he looked at it now.

"Take it easy, Wakeman," he begged. "What's riding you?"

"Kale killed Owen," Verl said in a dull voice. "If you have any idea where he could be, you'd better tell me now."

Dawson was a wreck of a man. He looked at death, and he knew it. "Oh God, Verl," he pleaded. "I don't know a damned thing about that. I haven't been out of my store since you left. And nobody's been here."

Perhaps the frantic entreaty reached Verl, for he lowered his gun. "Maybe you don't know," he conceded. "But if I learn you do, I'll be back. Bet on that."

He swept Dawson's face once more, turned, and strode out of the shop.

Dawson raised a shaky hand to wipe the sweat off his face after the door closed. He had better sit down before he fell down. He tottered to a chair and sank into it. The sweat kept coming, and he couldn't stop the shaking. He knew one thing for a certainty. He was glad he wasn't in Kale's boots. Kale was a dead man. It was written all over Verl's face. Dawson didn't know when or where it would happen, but it was as sure as the sun's rising tomorrow.

Outside, Verl paused before he mounted again. Dawson wasn't lying, he told himself. A man that scared wouldn't be clever enough to lie. Verl wanted to scream at his feeling of futility. He forced himself to remain calm and think rationally. This was only the first stop. There were a lot of other places in town where Kale could be.

South Pass wasn't a large town, but even so, it took time to search every possible hiding place. Verl visited every saloon, every hotel, every store. To his questions, he received the same negative answers. No one had seen Kale or Kyle, or had the slightest idea where they could be.

Verl was bone-tired as he made his last stop at a livery stable. He had been here before, and Grimley, the owner, started shaking his head the moment he saw Verl. "I told you before, I haven't seen him, Verl. He hasn't been here since you've been gone."

"I know that," Verl replied wearily. "I want to rent a horse. I won't return it until tomorrow."

"Take all the time you want," Grimley said. He only knew he wasn't comfortable when this man with the haunted eyes was around. Verl led the rented horse back to the Faber house. He shook his head at the questioning look on Ann's and Cleatis' faces.

"I looked all over," he said heavily. "Not a sign of him."

"Does that mean—" Ann started. She couldn't finish the question.

Verl could guess at what she wanted to know. "I'll never stop looking for Kale," he said savagely. "Until I know he's dead."

Ann shuddered at the intensity in Verl's voice. He was tearing himself apart inwardly, and that was the worst kind of grief.

"You haven't eaten?" she asked.

Verl shook his head. "I'm not hungry. I've got to get Owen back to Jabez." Just thinking of the blow he was going to deliver to the crippled old man was a shattering thought. But it had to be done, and he was the only one to do it.

"Stay at least for coffee," she begged. "It won't take me a minute to prepare it."

"No, Ann," he said gently. "I'll be all right." He pressed her arm before he walked over to where Owen lay. The inward crying was flooding over him again. Oh God, just a short while ago, Owen had been alive and vibrant.

He reached down and lifted Owen in his arms. He paused before he stepped out of the house. "Thanks for everything," he said in a lifeless voice.

He stared at Ann and shook his head. She was going to cry again, and he couldn't stand that.

Chapter Sixteen

Verl tied Owen's body onto the rented horse. He mounted heavily and started the dreaded trip back home.

He rode slowly. The day would be waning by the time he reached home. All the rebellious thoughts clashed and warred within his head. Owen so loved this time of year. He had reached only the beginning of the spring, not its fulfillment.

Verl angrily shook his head. These kinds of thoughts weren't doing him any good. He couldn't undo what had happened. But despite his protests, the thoughts kept crowding back into his mind. He relived all the times he and Owen had spent together, and they were many, for rarely did one go anyplace without the other.

He tried to throw back all the rebellious whys, knowing he couldn't answer them.

He knew the rebellion would remain long after the raw wound eased down a little. Maybe killing Kale would further ease the hurt. He hoped so, he thought fiercely. No matter how long it took, or where the quest took him, he would hunt Kale down.

Jabez must have seen him turn into the long lane that led up to the house, for he was outside when Verl rode up.

Jabez had seen the dangling body, and the knowledge of who it was, was in his frantic eyes. "It's not Owen," he said hoarsely, as if the denial would make it true.

Verl slid to the ground. He placed an arm about Jabez's shoulders. "Yes, Pa. Kale killed him. He and Owen got into an argument over Etta. Owen wasn't armed. That didn't matter to Kale. He shot Owen twice."

Jabez's face was a pale, frozen mask. "Did you look for him? You didn't let him get away with this?"

"I tried, Pa," Verl said wearily. "I searched for him every place he might be in town. I guess he's run for good this time."

Jabez misread the weariness for weakness. "You're not giving up?" he cried. "I want him killed." He was shaking with suppressed fury. "Kale's no longer my son."

"I look at him the same way," Verl replied. "He's not my brother. No, I'm not giving up. But I had to bring Owen home, didn't I?"

Jabez recognized the plea in Verl's voice. "Sure you did, son," he said gently. "Do you need help to bring him inside?"

"I can manage," Verl replied.

He carried Owen inside and laid him on the old battered sofa. Tears were stinging his eyes again, as he turned and walked into the kitchen.

"I can fix something to eat, Verl," Jabez offered.

Verl shook his head. "Not hungry, Pa. Maybe I could take a cup of coffee."

He sat at the table, staring mutely ahead as Jabez bustled about the old stove. He heard all the familiar sounds, the breaking of sticks to start a fire, the crackling of the fire. Owen used to sit here and listen to those same sounds.

Verl impatiently shook his head. This kind of thinking wasn't going to do him any good. He had to look ahead; the past was gone.

Jabez came to the table carrying the pot of coffee. He poured two cups and sat across from Verl. "What are your plans, Verl?" he asked quietly.

"I'll bury Owen in the morning," Verl said in clipped tones. "I'll start figuring then." As an explanation he added: "It's a big country out there. I don't want to start blind. I want to have a definite trace of Kale before I set out."

"That could take months," Jabez said in dismay.

"Yes," Verl answered simply. "I promise you one thing. However long it takes, I'll find him." He hoped that promise would assuage some of Jabez's agony.

They sat there a long time without speaking. Even though they didn't talk, they needed companionship desperately and dreaded to go to bed, for a sleepless night would surely follow.

In the morning Verl dug a grave. Jabez had offered to help and, almost roughly, Verl had ordered him away. He wanted to save Jabez all he could from this burden of grief.

The grave was dug and Verl was in the barn, nailing a crude coffin together. He worked furiously, hoping the physical activity would erase some of the hurt. His back was toward the door, but he sensed somebody come into the barn.

He turned, a frown beginning on his face. No matter how kind people's intentions were, Verl didn't want any company today.

The frown smoothed out as he saw Travis.

"Morning, Sam," he said flatly.

Travis nodded somberly. "I went through South Pass this morning, Verl. I heard what happened. Everybody's talking about it."

Verl nodded, but didn't comment.

"I'm sorry as hell, Verl." Travis was uncomfortable,

and he kept pulling at his fingers. "Anything I can do, Verl?"

Verl stared at him. Travis meant that. "There is, Sam. I need help carrying the coffin and lowering it into the ground. I don't think Jabez would be up to it."

"I'm only too glad to oblige," Travis said. His eyes touched Verl's, then slid away. The moment had too much stress for either man to be comfortable.

Verl and Travis carried the coffin out to the grave. With ropes they lowered the coffin into the ground. Verl looked at Jabez and Travis and asked, "Does anybody want to say anything?" He felt one of them should, but he was so choked up he would never get the words out.

One glance at Jabez told him that Jabez was in the same shape.

After a moment of awkward silence, Travis said, "Maybe I could say something."

Verl's sigh was heartfelt. "Be obliged to you, Sam."

Travis stood at the grave's edge and tugged off his hat. He looked up into the sky and said in a barely audible voice: "Lord, take the best care you can of him. He was a good boy. A lot of people are going to miss him." He stopped and looked helplessly at Verl. "I ain't no preacher," he mumbled.

"You did just fine," Verl said quietly. He fell to shoveling the dirt into the grave. The sooner this was done, the sooner this bad moment would fade from their minds.

Verl finished and said, "Come on in and have some coffee, Sam . . ."

"I'll run you people out of coffee if I keep on dropping by like this," Travis said and half smiled.

"Remind me to worry about that on the next trip you make." Verl owed Travis a lot. If he hadn't come by, he didn't know how he would have accomplished the burying.

The three sat at the table, sipping at their coffee. "We might as well talk about it," Travis said practically. "It's on everybody's mind."

Jabez sighed, but he looked at Travis, clear-eyed. "Verl and I talked about it a little while last night. Verl

97

promised me he wouldn't stop looking for Kale until he ran him down."

Verl nodded a curt affirmation. "I looked all over South Pass yesterday. Nobody had seen him." His eyes sparked with a new curiosity. "You haven't said why you happened to pick this time to come by."

"I thought I might give you a hand," Travis answered quietly.

Verl's face momentarily darkened. This was a family affair, and he wasn't seeking any outside help.

Travis sensed the coming refusal and said in a placating voice: "Maybe things have changed some, Verl. Maybe enough for you to welcome some help."

Verl looked sharply at him. Travis had something on his mind. "Go on," he said shortly.

"Kale and Kyle left with Butch Cassidy and his bunch last night."

The information jerked Verl's head up. "You're sure?"

"About as sure as any man can be," Travis answered. "Sanderson was late getting back from a hunting trip. It was after dark. He had almost gotten back to South Pass when he saw a pretty good sized bunch of horsemen coming toward him. He didn't know who they were, and he thought it smart to pull off the road and let them pass. He hoped they hadn't noticed him. The moon was pretty strong. Sanderson recognized Cassidy and some of the others." Travis nodded solemnly. "Kale and Kyle were riding with the bunch. Etta was with them."

Verl nodded. "Which way did they go, Sam?"

"South. I doubt if they'll stray very far off the out-laws' trail."

Verl's fist was clenched so tightly that he felt the bite of his nails in his palm. Cassidy's bunch had a head start, but at least he had a direction.

"You can't go after them alone," Travis said flatly.

Verl glared at him. "What's going to stop me?"

"Common sense, I hope," Travis replied. "One man couldn't get very far up against that gang. I don't know what Kale told Cassidy, but Cassidy took them in. I'd say you'd be smart to use all the help you can get. I talked to a Pinkerton Detective Agency man, Dan Welles. The Pinks usually handle such affairs for the Union Pacific. He told me the railroad is pretty upset about that car that was blown up."

Maybe there will be no better time to clear up something. Verl spoke up quietly: "Sam, when you were here and asking about that train robbery, I misled you. You asked me if the twins could handle dynamite, and I said it was impossible. Then I remembered Kale might know enough to pull off that job. He was only twelve when Pa and I blew out some rocks." He glanced at his father. "Remember, Pa?"

Jabez nodded, his eyes blazing. "I remember. He asked a thousand questions. Dynamite seemed to fascinate him. But I would never have connected it with what happened."

"I didn't either, until I got to thinking about it," Verl said. He glanced at Travis. "Sorry, Sam."

Travis' eyes were reproachful. "So am I, Verl. We might have cut him off before—" He couldn't finish the sentence.

"What do you think I'm thinking about?" Verl asked half-angrily. "I've been blaming myself ever since Owen was shot."

Travis shook his head. The gesture was recrimination enough. "Can't change what's done, Verl," he said practically. "Do you want to hear the rest of what Welles told me?"

Verl still seethed in his self-blame. "Go ahead," he growled.

"Seven more Pinkerton men will be in South Pass in the morning. I'm riding with them. Do you want to go?"

"Hell, yes, I want to go," Verl shouted.

"It'll be a long, hard trip," Travis warned. "And I don't know how long it will take. But that many men would have a better chance of success than a lone one."

"I'm going," Verl said firmly. He glanced at Jabez, and a new worry occurred to him. Jabez would be left alone here, and he couldn't handle the chores that would come up.

"Don't you hesitate because of me," Jabez said

sternly. "I want to see Kale run down as bad as you do."

Verl stood and reached for his sheepskin. "I'm going over to see Tom Anderson. He's got two strapping boys. Maybe he can see fit to lend us one of them."

"You don't have to because of me," Jabez shouted after him as he went out the door.

"Always was hardheaded," Jabez fumed as the door closed.

Travis grinned at him. "But a good hardheadedness. Comes in handy in a time like this."

"Well, maybe," Jabez conceded.

Verl was gone an hour. He came in, looking more relaxed. "Talked to Tom," he announced. "Tom's pleased to do what he can. He's sending Carl over in the morning, to stay as long as you need him."

"Wasn't necessary," Jabez grumbled.

"But it makes it a lot easier on all of us," Verl said quietly. He looked at Travis. "Did he say anything about me being hardheaded?"

Travis nodded. "How'd you know that?"

"Just figured he would. Now do you know where I get that hardheadedness?"

He walked over to the gun rack on the wall and took down a rifle.

"That's Owen's new rifle. He bought it last year."

Verl looked squarely at his father. "Can you think of a better purpose I can put it to?"

Jabez sighed. "No, I guess not."

"Sam, I'm ready to leave whenever you are," Verl said.

"First thing in the morning," Travis said. "No use rushing it. It won't be done in a day, or even two."

Verl fretted at the thought of the delay. But Travis was right. Losing his patience could cost a man far more than he could ever gain. "In the morning, then," he said.

Chapter Seventeen

Etta groaned as Kale helped her to the ground.

"Tired, baby?" he asked.

She clung tightly to him for a moment. "I'm so stiff," she complained.

"You're not sorry you came?" he asked anxiously.

"Never," she answered emphatically. "For the first time in a long while, I feel alive." Her voice lowered as she said, "The women don't like me much."

Kale glanced at the other four women who were with the bunch. He didn't know any of them by name. "Just jealous of you," he said and grinned. "None of them as pretty as you."

Etta planted a quick kiss on his cheek. "You're prejudiced. But I do wish they liked me more. I tried to talk to them on the other two rest stops. They treated me like I had a disease." Etta grimaced at the memory.

"Work on them," Kale advised. "You can win them over."

Etta nodded. "Maybe I can offer to help prepare supper."

"That's the trick," Kale said with hearty approval.

Etta's face brightened as a thought hit her. "Kale, could I give one of those dresses to Nettie?" She saw she had lost him. "I know all their names," she said complacently. "Nettie is Kid Curry's woman. She's the big raw-boned one. I think she bosses the others. If I can make her like me, maybe it'll influence the others. I'd like to get along with all of them."

"Sure, you can," Kale said in instant approval. "Take any of the dresses you want." He walked away, intent upon joining the other men. He enjoyed just listening to what they had to say. These men were all legendary characters, and each one had left his mark on the West.

Etta stood a moment in indecision, not quite sure what her approach should be. She timidly approached Nettie, who was opening saddlebags and pulling out pots and packages of food.

"Anything I can do to help?" Etta ventured.

Nettie glanced at her out of hooded eyes. "If there is, I'll tell you," she snapped.

Etta sighed. Nettie wasn't going to be easy to win over. "But I'd like to do something," she persisted.

Nettie looked squarely at her, and her animosity was naked and pulsing. "Just keep out of my way," she said fiercely.

Etta determinedly stood her ground. "Why don't you like me?"

"Why should I?" Nettie growled. "I've seen you making sheep eyes at my man."

For a moment, Etta was startled at the absurdity of the accusation, then she smiled inwardly. "I haven't, honestly," she said. "I've got all I can do to keep Kale interested. I've been in love with him ever since we met several months ago. I didn't think I had a chance until he asked me to go with him."

Nettie's crusty exterior melted a little. "Your first love, huh? It grips a woman pretty hard. If you want to help, gather up some firewood and start a fire."

Etta's face was shining as she turned away. She was winning, and she knew it.

Etta gathered wood and built a fire. Before lighting it, she circled the wood with stones so the fire couldn't spread.

Nettie nodded gruff approval. "You're a good worker," she said grudgingly. "Bring me some water. The creek's right down there." She pointed to her left.

Etta nodded eagerly, picked up two buckets, and hurried to the creek. Nettie's hard shell was melting. Before this night was over, Nettie would have an entirely different opinion of her.

Etta sat close to Nettie during the meal. "Good cooking," she said, and meant it.

Nettie thawed at the unexpected praise. "I wasn't born with looks," she said pensively. "But the one thing I can do is cook. Maybe it's enough to keep a man's interest."

"It is, Nettie. Kid Curry would be a fool to ever think of letting you go."

Nettie sighed. "I hope you're right," she murmured. "Sometimes I wonder—" She broke off and was lost in thought, then finally asked: "What made you join up with the bunch? It's a rough life for a woman, with few pleasures. Maybe a few dollars to spend occasionally. But mostly it's strain and constant worry. I had another man before I met Kid Curry."

Etta caught the wistful note in her voice. "Something happen to him?"

"A lawman's bullet stopped him," Nettie said flatly. "For a long time, I didn't think I'd ever get over it." She shrugged. "I found out life goes on."

She stared into the dying coals of the fire, lost again in her reveries.

Etta thought this was a good time to finish winning Nettie over. She slipped away, moved to the dress case and opened it. The moonlight was strong enough to see what she was doing. She knew all these dresses well, and she selected a green one, thinking the color would go well with Nettie's red hair.

She came back with the dress and handed it to Nettie. "I want you to have this, Nettie."

Nettie was astounded, and she breathed faster. "It's beautiful. But why?"

"You were kind to me," Etta said simply. "I was pretty lonesome, and you talked to me."

Nettie studied her for so long that Etta began to fear she would turn her down. "I want you to have it," she said eagerly. "If it doesn't fit, I could alter it. I'm pretty good with a needle."

"You're all right," Nettie said roughly. She stood and looked across the dying fire. The other three women

103

had chosen to eat by themselves, plainly displaying their dislike for Etta. "I'll be right back," Nettie said. "I want to straighten something out."

Her strides were long, almost mannish, as she strode around the fire. Etta saw Nettie join the three women, but she couldn't hear what she was saying. But those three listened. Their faces were intense. Nettie was a force among the women in this bunch.

Nettie came back and sat down beside Etta. "I told them I had you all wrong," Nettie said gruffly. "I told them from now on to treat you right, or they'd have me to answer to. You won't have any more trouble from them."

"I'm grateful," Etta whispered. "I do so want to stay with Kale." "You will, you will," Nettie assured her. Her face softened with eagerness. "Do you suppose sometime tomorrow you can fix the dress to fit?"

"Count on it," Etta said happily.

She found Kale and slipped under the blanket with him. He didn't seem too happy to see her, and his voice was sulky. "You sure stayed away from me tonight. You didn't even come over for supper."

Etta laughed deep in her throat as she wrapped her arms about his neck. "I was only doing what you told me to," she said serenely. "Making friends with Nettie."

Kale's sulkiness disappeared. "Think you succeeded?"

"I know I did." She kissed him long and hard.

"Sure you're not sorry you came?" Kale asked anxiously.

"Not any more. Not after Nettie and I got everything straightened out. I'm going to like this life, Kale." Excitement crept into her voice. "No one looking over my shoulder, nobody ordering me around." She kissed him again. "Doesn't this prove anything to you?"

His arms tightened about her, and he nuzzled her throat. "It sure does."

Cassidy seemed in no hurry to make time down the outlaw trail. Kale rode beside him. He wasn't worried about the slowness of their progress any more. He felt entirely secure. Cassidy and the others had accepted him and Kyle. He wasn't sure how Kyle felt. Several times he had seen Kyle moping along, his face dejected. Kyle might already be regretting joining Cassidy. Kale snorted at the thought. That was just too damned bad. He didn't give a damn what Kyle felt, or what he thought. Kale knew he'd made a smart move for both of them.

"Seems like the women are getting along just fine," Cassidy remarked. "At breakfast they were chattering together like a bunch of hens. I don't mind telling you, I didn't know how introducing a new woman would work out, but everything's fine."

Kale beamed. "Etta's quite a gal for making friends."

Cassidy turned in his saddle to look back at the string of riders following them. "She sure is," he agreed heartily.

Kale wondered if Verl was looking for them. But surely, Verl wouldn't be fool enough to come after him when he was with Cassidy. But what if he didn't know? What if he just came blundering after them?

Kale scowled ferociously. If that should happen, Verl could be stopped the same way Owen was stopped. Kale no longer felt a sense of belonging to a family. If he had any family at all, it was right here in this bunch.

"What's chewing on you?" Cassidy asked. "The way you look, it doesn't taste very good."

"Just thinking," Kale muttered. "Trying to sort out some things in my mind."

"Thinking we're not making enough time?" Cassidy asked.

Kale flushed. He didn't want Cassidy to think he was critical of him. "Lord, no, Butch," he said. He had dropped the "Mister Cassidy" hours ago. "I was just wondering if you're heading any particular place."

Cassidy chuckled. "Eager to get started, huh? I'll tell you and the others my plans tomorrow."

Kale felt his excitement mount. By the glint in Cassidy's eyes, Cassidy had something definite in mind. Kale wanted to get to work as soon as possible. He had money, but that wouldn't last forever. He wanted to make a lot of money and lay it before Etta. He wanted to prove she hadn't chosen wrong when she picked him. Every time he thought of last night, his face heated and he tingled all over.

Cassidy gathered the bunch around him after breakfast in the morning. "Funds beginning to run a little low," he said casually. "Time to do something about it."

Kale saw the exchange of nods between the men who knew Cassidy best, and their eyes picked up a new fire. Evidently, they sensed that Cassidy had picked out a new target.

"We're about fifteen miles out of Rock Springs," Cassidy said. "But I don't want to get there until tomorrow."

"Why?" Curry asked. "We could easily make it today."

Cassidy impatiently shook his head. "Tomorrow's the first of the month. Payday for all the coal miners around Rock Springs. I'm going to ride in today and see if I can learn which bank handles the payrolls and where it's located. I haven't got the slightest idea of what it will amount to, but it should be a nice little heap."

Men whooped and pounded each other on the back. Old Butch was thinking again. He never missed a trick. He looked after them real good. Just when things were getting a little slow, Butch came up with a plan of action.

Cassidy's grin broadened at the vociferous approval. He held up his hand to quiet them. "Hold it. I want to say something else."

He waited until he had their attention before going on. "Take it easy until I get back. I'll know then exactly what we're going to do."

"Everybody going?" Curry asked.

Cassidy gave the question a brief consideration. "We don't need the whole bunch for a little job like this. Five

106

of us should handle it just fine." He looked over at Kale and Kyle. "How'd you two like to go along and break in?"

"Wouldn't like anything better," Kale exclaimed. Kyle nodded, but there was reluctance in the gesture.

Kale watched Cassidy ride away. He was damned lucky he had gotten into this bunch. He thought of what might have faced him if Cassidy hadn't taken him in, and a small shiver ran through him.

Cassidy came back before dark. He called the bunch around him. The women never tried to horn in on serious business.

"I found out which bank it is," Cassidy announced. "It sits on an alley that runs clear through to the next street. The bank is on the main street, but that could be to our advantage. More people to get mixed up in the confusion a bank robbery creates. We'll leave the horses headed down the alley and go out the back way. Five men will be enough." He pointed at Harry Longabaugh, more familiarly known as the Sundance Kid. "Harry, you and Curry will ride in with me. Kale and Kyle will make up the five."

Kale looked surreptitiously around the seated circle of men. He expected to see rage and disappointment show on their faces for being left out. To his surprise, every face remained placid, and he didn't hear a single dissenting word.

Ben Kilpatrick, known as the Tall Texan, spit into the dust ahead of him. "Suits me just fine. I don't have to ride my ass off, and I share just the same."

Cassidy grinned at him. "You've got it, Ben."

Now Kale understood the secret of Cassidy's success. He ran this bunch with strict discipline and fairness. Men understood that and went along with his orders.

"We'll be leaving about six in the morning," Cassidy said, and the meeting broke up.

Kyle rode with Kale to Rock Springs in the morning. "You scared, Kale?" Kyle asked.

"Naw," Kale said, and meant it. Why should he be frightened? He was riding with Butch Cassidy, and Cassidy was a mastermind. Nothing was going to happen to them. "You scared, Kyle?"

"Maybe a little," Kyle confessed. He said quickly, at Kale's frown, "I was more scared in the stagecoach robbery."

A grin replaced Kale's frown. "It looks like you're improving, Kyle. I wish Butch had given us more important jobs. All we're going to do is hold the horses."

"I ain't complaining," Kyle said.

Cassidy stopped the group just outside of Rock Springs. He pulled out a watch and looked at it. "Made good time. We'll go in one at a time and meet in the alley. You can't miss it. All set?" He looked at each man in turn, then nodded. "Let's get started. Curry, you go ahead. Just act casual."

"Why, I was thinking of riding in, carrying a big sign saying BANK ROBBERY COMING."

Cassidy chuckled. "Get going," he said easily.

Kale and Kyle were the last two to ride into the alley. Kale felt his heart pounding.

Cassidy instructed Kale and Kyle which way to head the horses. "The three of us will go into the bank one at a time. When the third one arrives, we go into action. Make it fast. I want to be in and out in a few minutes."

He was satisfied that his instructions were understood. He dropped off his horse and walked easily to the mouth of the alley, turned to his left, and disappeared.

Longabaugh went next, and Curry last.

Kale envied every one of them. They looked so assured, so at ease.

Kyle was struck by that easy assurance too, for he remarked: "Lord, Kale, none of them bothered to put on a mask."

"I guess they figure they're already well-known. Knowing who they are ain't the main thing."

"What is, Kale?"

Kale winked at him. "They've got to catch them. Nobody ain't done that yet."

He sat there, fidgeting in his saddle. God, how time dragged. Each passing minute seemed an eternity.

The pressure of waiting was getting to Kyle too, for he said: "Kale, ain't they been gone a long time?"

"Only a few minutes," Kale assured him, but he was frowning. Had something gone wrong? He jerked his head around at the dull, flat report of a pistol. That came from the bank. He groaned deep in his throat. Something had gone wrong.

He shook his head at the frantic inquiry in Kyle's face. Hell, he couldn't tell him what to do. He guessed all they could do was wait.

He flinched as he heard another shot. All hell must have broken loose in the bank.

"Shouldn't we get out of here?" Kyle begged.

"No," Kale snapped. "We were told to wait here, and we do just exactly that." He hurt from the pressure of the mounting tension. If only he knew what was going on.

Longabaugh came around the corner into the alley, and he was running. He carried a canvas sack in one hand, his pistol in the other.

Kyle handed him the reins of his horse, and Longabaugh mounted. "The other two will be here any second," he panted.

Curry came next, and he, too, carried a canvas sack.

Kale kept his head turned toward the mouth of the alley. Where was Cassidy? He flinched as he heard another shot. Oh God, they had Cassidy pinned in the bank.

Longabaugh saw the wildness grip Kale's face, and he guessed its source. "Just hold it where you are. Butch can take care of himself."

Kale's sigh was a long, tearing sound, but Longabaugh's words had their calming influence. There wasn't a damned thing he could do but wait.

Cassidy ran into the alley the next instant. Like the other two, he carried a canvas sack. His face was hard and grim, but otherwise, he didn't look particularly concerned.

Cassidy ran straight at his horse's rear.

Kale watched him, big-eyed. What was Cassidy

doing? If he didn't slow up soon, he was going to run squarely into his horse.

Cassidy answered Kale's unspoken question in a hurry. He slowed his pace a fraction and vaulted into the air. His boots must have springs in them, for he catapulted over the horse's rump and landed in the saddle.

Kale flipped him the reins, and Cassidy caught them. He spurred his horse hard, and the others followed suit. Five men raced down the alley. Kale's shoulders felt pinched together in fearful anticipation of a slug.

But Kale didn't hear a gun's report. The people were still held by the confusion in the bank, and they didn't know which direction Cassidy and the others had taken. The five men reached the end of the alley, Kale riding just behind Cassidy.

Cassidy swung to the right, and the others followed.

They passed people on the street, and Kale got a quick, confused impression of open mouths in shocked faces. But evidently, nobody knew what was going on, for no one made an effort to stop them.

Cassidy kept the horses going at top speed until the town was well behind him. He kept looking back, but he must not have seen anything threatening, for he became more relaxed.

Then he held up his hand and slowed, and the others pulled up around him.

"The horses need a breather," Cassidy said. "We're safe enough for a few minutes."

Kale took the opportunity to congratulate Cassidy on the way he had vaulted into his saddle. "Neatest trick I ever saw," he said with fervor.

Cassidy barely glanced at him, and his face was foreboding. Something other than Kale's praise was on his mind, but he took time to say absently: "Been working with this horse the last couple of years to teach him to hold still. I figured it might come in handy."

He patted the horse's neck. "First time I ever used it. You did real well, boy."

Cassidy turned his head and glowered at Curry. "Damn you, Kid. You started all that mess inside, and two men were killed." His face twisted at the thought.

"What the hell was I going to do?" Curry asked in aggrieved tones. "I saw that bank officer reach into his desk. I supposed it was a move for a gun. Damn it, Butch, I warned all of them not to make a move. You heard me."

"Your hasty action encouraged a teller to try the same stunt. I waited until I saw the gun in his hand before I shot him. I still say, you could have handled it differently."

"I didn't see it that way," Curry said curtly. "We got out all right, didn't we?"

Cassidy nodded grim agreement. "But this time we pulled more attention to us. They'll look harder for the ones who killed two men."

Kale frowned puzzledly. "I thought I heard three shots."

Cassidy grinned bleakly. "You did. I fired a third shot into the ceiling just before I left. The last thing I saw was people diving for the floor. I figured it'd give us a few more seconds."

Kale looked back along the empty road. "You sure figured right," he said. "I'll bet they haven't recovered yet."

The coldness left Cassidy's eyes at the praise. "You did all right too. You held your place when those shots could have put you into a run. My God, what a mess we would have been in if you bolted at the first shot."

"I only did what you told me to," Kale said. He tried to keep from grinning. He felt as though that would be accepted as a form of bragging.

"Well, it's done," Cassidy said heavily. "We'd better get moving again. Look for a long, hard chase," he warned.

He set his horse at a fast trot, and the others followed him. Kale thought about the scene in the bank as he rode. He couldn't see where Curry had any blame coming to him. He would have done just the same, if some fool had made the same unwise movement.

He was thinking about it when they rode into camp.

He jumped off and grabbed Etta in his arms. "It was a big success," he crowed. "Came off without a hitch." That wasn't quite true, but there was no use worrying Etta with details. Time enough to speak of that if a search developed.

"How much did you get, Kale?" Etta was breathless.

"I don't know yet," he replied carelessly. "We didn't take time to do any counting. I think Butch is going to do that now."

Men were gathering around Cassidy, their greed avid in their eyes. This time, there was no objection to the women joining them. They were entitled to see the fruits of a rough and dangerous life.

Cassidy opened the first canvas sack and pulled out a handful of money. He kept dipping into the sack and adding to the growing pile before him.

"I don't see how you gathered up that much money in such a short time," Kale said. "You weren't in there that long."

Cassidy was emptying the second sack. "We hit it lucky," he said soberly. "They were just opening the vault when we came in. All we had to do was go inside and start grabbing."

He kept adding to the ever-increasing pile. He opened the third sack and added the contents of it to the pile of money.

Cassidy finished counting and looked up. "We made one hell of a haul," he announced solemnly. "I make it a little over thirty-five thousand dollars."

Men danced and pounded each other on the back. Their faces were greasy with the shine of elation.

Kale looked at the pile of money, almost sick with envy. Cassidy had six men in his bunch when Kale and Kyle joined it. Even though they had taken part in the holdup, it was only a minor part. They couldn't reasonably expect an equal share of the money.

Cassidy counted out the money into nine piles. As far as Kale could see, the piles were equal.

"You're giving us an equal part?" he asked in a choked voice.

Cassidy shrugged. "Why not? You were in on it. I've

always operated on the principle that everybody shares alike. Keeps down a hell of a lot of jealousy."

Kale's hand was shaking as he pocketed his share. By his rough figuring, he had something just under four thousand dollars. Jubilation welled up in him, and he wanted to shout.

He took Etta's hand and led her away from the crowd.

"Don't go too far," Cassidy called after him. "We're leaving after a short rest. We've got a long ride ahead of us."

Kale waited until he was out of earshot of the others. "Did you hear what went on back there?" he asked.

"Not all of it, Kale. I know Butch gave you some money." She couldn't keep the hard ring out of her voice as she asked, "How much was it?"

Kale pulled the money from his pocket and stuffed it down into the bosom of her dress. "You can count it," he said, grinning. "Then you can tell me how much it is. Butch gave me and Kyle equal shares."

She reached down into her bosom, and her small hand was filled with money when it reappeared. She kept dipping between her breasts, coming out with more and more money.

"Oh, Kale," she squealed. "All this money." She threw her arms about his neck. "And you asked me if I was sorry I left with you." She kissed him over and over. "You can do anything you want at any time."

"This time I'll have to put it off," he said huskily. "But I'll make up for it later."

Chapter Eighteen

Eight men were talking to Sanderson when Verl and Travis walked into the general store in the morning.

Travis introduced Verl to Dan Welles, a short, blocky man with a heavy, brooding face. Welles either wasn't feeling well, or he had soured on life early. It could be the latter, Verl thought. His line of business brought him in constant contact with the seamier phases of living.

Verl shook Welles's hand, and Travis said: "Welles will have to introduce the others. I don't know all of them myself."

Verl met tall and short men, heavy men, and some slat-thin. They were nothing alike in physical appearance, but there was the same quiet assurance in each of them. Maybe it's competence, Verl thought, the assurance of knowing their job and doing it well. He gave up trying to keep all these names catalogued in his mind. He would learn those names through association, and he was afraid the association was going to be a long one.

"Verl Wakeman," one of the men murmured. "I heard a strange story about two of your brothers joining up with Cassidy's bunch."

"Twin brothers," he said flatly. "I think they were the two who held up your train. One of those twins killed my brother."

It was a simple, unimpassioned statement, yet it said it all. It told these listening men of the wrenching loss Verl had suffered. Verl's fists were clenched, and he forced them open. "When Sam told me about you boys going after the twins, I decided I was going too."

Welles nodded sympathetically. "It could be a long chase," he warned. "And a tough one."

"I don't give a damn if it leads clear into Mexico." For the first time, emotion shook Verl's voice.

Welles's eyes were troubled. He had heard there was never a worse hate than that between brothers. He might learn if the old saying was true. "Why do you think your brothers joined up with Cassidy's bunch?"

Verl had complete control again. "I think they knew they'd better," he said calmly. "Kale and Kyle knew I'd hunt them down. How they prevailed on Cassidy to take them, I don't know."

"That's going to make it a lot tougher," Welles said and sighed. "We weren't after Cassidy in particular, though there's a dozen crimes against him. But your brothers will profit from riding with him."

"I imagine," Verl said levelly. He hadn't been up against Cassidy personally, but he had heard many a tale about him. "But we know which direction they're going, and they won't stray far off the outlaw trail, will they?"

"No," Welles said soberly. "But, my God, man, do you know what that trail covers?"

"I've heard something of it," Verl said bleakly. Evidently, Welles knew the trail from personal experience. That could be a tremendous help.

"Six hundred miles, stretching from Montana to Mexico," Welles mused. "And Cassidy knows every foot of it. He knows all the water holes and the springs. A man without that knowledge can die of thirst or starve to death along that trail."

"But you know it too," Verl challenged.

"Not as well as Cassidy," Welles replied gloomily. "Cassidy knows every shelter along that trail. I've seen dozens of crude cabins and sandstone caves. It'll take a lot of searching to cover every one of them. We know the general direction they took. We'll hear rumors of their passing. That's about all we can hope for right now." He turned to Sanderson and pulled a long list from his pocket. "We need supplies," he stated. His face twisted. "God, we'll be sick of eating out of cans before this is over."

"Well, we're agreed on one point," Verl drawled. "It's going to be a long, hard chase."

Welles grimaced. "That's about it." He turned his attention to reading off the supplies he wanted.

Verl watched Sanderson scurry about the store, adding items to the ever-growing pile. All those supplies were going to take several pack horses. He didn't comment, for he knew Welles had taken care of that. From now on, he would be a listener and observer until they ran down Cassidy and the twins.

It was nearly noon before the long string of riders and pack horses headed out of town. Verl rode beside Travis.

"Getting too old for this kind of nonsense," Travis complained. "What do you think of them?"

"Favorably," Verl said gravely. "They seem to know what they're doing."

The posse moved slowly ever southward. The season had advanced enough so that all of the snow was gone, and the hills showed their normal color, gray-brown. Only in the higher elevations were there caps of white on the highest peaks. Verl thought they could expect to find snow in Colorado and Utah, but after that, the country would turn hot and dry.

Even though it was only a half day's ride, Verl was glad when the day ended. He stepped down from the saddle and moved slowly about, trying to work the stiffness out of his joints. He could bet that Travis' old joints were giving him hell.

Welles built up a big fire and, at Verl's raising eyebrows, said: "It won't be seen. At least, by the wrong eyes. They've got a long lead on us. I don't expect to hear anything of them for several more days. If we're that lucky," he finished with a growl.

Verl nodded and moved closer to the warmth of the fire. It was supposed to be spring, but the night air still had a bite.

He watched Welles open cans and pour their contents into pans. His face was absorbed in his cooking, and Verl thought, he likes doing this.

Welles felt Verl's scrutiny and looked up. "The boys know of my hobby," Welles said. "I like to cook." That could have been a defensive statement. "They elected me to do all the cooking on this trip."

"Good thing you're along," Verl observed. "I'd hate to think what you boys would be eating if I was doing the cooking." He doubtfully shook his head. "But it's a hell of a lot of work for one man."

Welles chuckled. "You don't think I'd be dumb enough to take on this chore without making some arrangements. I only do the cooking. The rest of you gather the firewood, build the fire, and wash the dishes. I might help with the packing because I like to know where things are, but that's my limit."

Verl's eyes gleamed. "I'm getting more respect for you every minute."

"You'd better," Welles threatened. "I'm doing your cooking."

Verl sat spraddle-legged while he ate with relish. Welles turned out one hell of a meal, considering the crude conditions under which he worked. Every now and then, Verl glanced over at Welles and nodded.

He took another spoonful of stew. "We sure won't starve," he said to Travis, sitting beside him.

Travis didn't finish all his stew. "Too damned tired to eat," he sighed.

"I'll finish it for you," Verl offered.

Travis handed him the tin plate. "I keep thinking of all the days ahead," he said and groaned. "They'll only be more of the same, but tougher."

Verl clucked sympathetically.

Welles topped the meal off with canned peaches. Verl picked up Travis' plate and utensils and joined the others, washing their dishes at the nearby creek.

"Fine meal," he said heartily when Welles came up.

"Just like to check that everything's clean," Welles said. "We're getting fairly close to the Utah line. Dry country there. We'll be washing dishes with sand there." He scowled at a clean plate. "I never feel sand gets the dishes as clean as water."

Verl nodded, but his thoughts were on the days ahead. "What's the next big town we come to?"

Welles reflected for a moment. "That should be Rock Springs. Maybe we can get some information there. If Cassidy and his bunch passed through there, somebody should have noticed them."

Verl nodded. "Just asking. Think I'll turn in."

Welles cocked an eye at him. "Did you bring a piece of tarpaulin?" At Verl's nod, he said: "Good. That sky looks like snow to me."

Verl thought of Travis having trouble already. A good snowfall would be all they needed.

Verl slept soundly. The first light awakened him, and he stretched and yawned. He looked in disbelief at the white covering of snow on his tarpaulin. That Welles was a good forecaster.

Travis sat up and cursed the snow passionately. "Anything to make it easier," he growled.

"Only a couple of inches," Verl said. "Could have been a hell of a lot worse."

Travis groused about the weather clear up to breakfast. Verl noticed he had picked up a hacking cough. A lot of old-timers seemed to have that malady.

Welles was a genius over a wood fire. He got his breakfast fire going despite damp wood, and he even served sourdough pancakes. A stack of those and two or three cups of coffee were just the solid, rib-sticking food to get a man going on a raw morning. Verl thought wistfully of the pancakes Jabez served. Already, it seemed as though home was far away. His seething hatred of Kale returned stronger than ever. Owen would never again see the home he so loved.

"What's your weather prediction for today?" he asked Welles.

Welles cocked an eye at the sky. "Storm's about over," he predicted. "That wasn't bad. Just a little skiff."

As they rode out, Verl looked back along the line of riders. Travis' face was a frozen mask. Verl couldn't tell what he was thinking. Travis would suffer to the bitter end. But not without his complaints, Verl thought and chuckled.

Welles called Verl's attention to a bluff of sandstone off to the right.

Verl peered at it intently, but he could see nothing

unusual about the bluff, just an unbroken expanse of rough rock.

Wells pointed. "There! Just below that gap near the top."

Verl peered until he made out what Welles saw. Gradually, the crumbling outlines of a weather-beaten and eroded shack came into view. "I see it," he said, and looked questioningly at Welles.

"It's an outlaw cabin," Welles said. "Once was occupied by Hank Myerson. He lived in it until he made a bad mistake. He stepped out of his door without being sure who was outside. Tom Horn was waiting for him. He cut him down."

Verl nodded. He had heard of the famous bounty hunter, though he had never seen him. "Never heard of this Myerson. What did he do?"

"Just a small-time outlaw," Welles replied. "He'd steal anything that wasn't nailed down. He kept at it until the rewards for him mounted up enough to interest Horn. I heard the bounty was several hundred dollars." He shook his head in sober reflection. "The things a man will do for a few dollars. That goes on both sides of the law. Hell of a way for a man to live out his life— lonely, running, and hiding. I wonder if Myerson would've changed, if he'd had the chance."

"I doubt it," Verl said flatly. "Did you ever hear of any of them changing?"

Welles shook his head. "Not very many."

"What happened to Horn?" Verl asked. "I never heard."

"He was hanged for the murder of a fourteen-year-old boy, a couple of years back, in Cheyenne. Some say Horn didn't do it."

"Were they right?"

Welles shrugged in sudden irritation. "Hell, I don't know. The judge said he did. I guess that's all that's necessary. It was in Tom's case, anyway."

They rode a way in silence, then Welles said, "I know if a man lives a violent life, he usually winds up the same way." He grinned bleakly. "I guess you could say I've lived a violent life. Maybe I'll wind up that way."

119

"Will you?"

"Lord, I hope not," Welles replied. "I guess it's a good thing a man can't see what's ahead of him. If he could, it'd scare the Jesus out of him. Or put it back in." He chuckled wryly. "I'm really wound up this morning. I only pointed out Myerson's old shack to show you how difficult they are to spot. The country's littered with that kind of wreck. We'll see dozens of them before we're done with this trip."

Verl nodded absently. Kale was headed for the same violent end Myerson knew. He wondered if it would have made any difference, if Kale knew how so many outlaws ended. Verl doubted it. Those examples were all around Kale, and it hadn't deterred him.

"We'll see Rock Springs before tomorrow's out," Welles said.

"Good. That shows we're making progress."

"Not too much," Welles said gloomily. "When I look at what's ahead, I can hardly see where we're moving at all."

Verl laughed wryly. "Talking to you isn't the most uplifting thing in the world."

"The wife says the same thing," Welles responded. "She says I get more crotchety every passing day."

They fell silent, each wrapped in his own thoughts. It was odd, but Verl hadn't thought of Welles and his kind having a family and loved ones. He wondered if all the outlaws, fleeing down the trail, had the same warm feelings for their families. Not Kale, he thought violently. Kale pitched all that out the door when he started on the outlaw trail. Wait a minute, he cautioned himself. He took Etta with him. Would she bring him any pleasure, he pondered. If so, it wouldn't be for long. That was a promise he had made to Owen.

Chapter Nineteen

Welles waited until the other riders crowded around him. "Rock Springs," he announced. "Probably the biggest town we'll see for some time." He frowned as a thought struck him. "I haven't the slightest idea how far we are behind Cassidy, but I don't think speed is going to do us any good at the moment." He looked at the others and grinned. "How'd you like to spend a night in a real bed and eat a meal in a restaurant? Let the railroad pay for it."

Welles's' proposal was met with heartfelt approval.

"Let's go, then," Welles said as he picked up the reins. "I'll pick the best-looking hotel I can find."

Verl dropped back beside Travis. "What do you think about what Welles said?"

"Saved my life," Travis said seriously. "Another night of sleeping on that cold ground, and I don't think I could have gotten up." He saw the twitching of Verl's lip corners and warned: "Don't you go laughing at me. I know one thing for certain. This is the last time I ever go on a trip like this, no matter what the reason."

Verl nodded soberly. He guessed Travis was hurting more than anybody could guess.

Welles led his string of riders down one street, then another. He passed up the first hotel they came to. Verl guessed he didn't like its looks.

Welles stopped before a more flashy building and swung down. "This looks like it could be all right. As long as we're letting the railroad pay for this, I want it to be the best we can find."

Men laughed and slapped their thighs. This was the kind of humor they could appreciate.

Welles grinned up at them. "I'll go in and see if they

can handle all of us and find out what's the best restaurant in town." He flicked his fingers under the brim of his hat and strode into the hotel.

Welles didn't come back out for quite a while, and the men began to fidget. "Hell, he must be trying to buy the damned hotel," somebody grumbled.

The sour humor pulled a smile from Verl, but he did wonder what was taking Welles so long.

Welles came back out, and his expression had completely changed. The lightheartedness of a few minutes ago was gone, for his face was stiff and foreboding.

"Did they throw you out, Welles?" someone called. "We don't have to stay here. We can find another place. These damned fancy hotels that turn a man down."

Welles shook his head, cutting into the man's tirade. "They didn't turn us down, Bill. The reason I took so long was that I was talking to the manager. He's still excited about what happened."

He was silent, pulling at his lower lip in reflection. He took so long that Harley said impatiently, "Will you tell us what happened?"

"The manager was making a deposit in the bank a few days ago. It was held up while he was in there. Two men killed while the robbery was going on. He said the last bandit out fired a shot into the ceiling. The manager hit the floor like everybody else."

"Who did it?" Harley asked. "Or did he know?"

Travis moved his horse nearer Welles. "Hell, that's easy to answer," he said in disgust. "It was Cassidy and his bunch, wasn't it?"

Welles nodded slowly. "Cassidy and two of his men."

Verl caught Welles's attention. "Could the manager describe them?"

Welles caught what Verl was driving at, and he shook his head. "But that doesn't prove the twins weren't along. Cassidy probably left some men outside the bank to cut off a possible attack or to hold horses. Cassidy usually breaks a man in, in a hurry. It gives him an opportunity to observe the caliber of the new men. They could have been with him, Verl."

"Did you ask how much they got?" Travis asked. He

seemed more alert, and the grayness wasn't as pronounced in his face.

"Over thirty-five thousand," Welles replied.

Travis whistled softly. "It was a big one. How far ahead of us are they?"

"Two full days. Maybe a little more."

"Do the local people know what direction they took?"

"Local posses went out after them. All of them are back. They followed tracks heading south. They lost the tracks in a rocky stretch of ground."

Travis swore. "Really eager to get after him, weren't they? I guess knowing who pulled off the robbery dampened their enthusiasm." His shoulders slumped, and he looked dejected. "There goes that sleeping in a real bed. We've got to get after them."

"That's about it, Sam," Welles said. "At least we've got definite proof they're operating in this part of the country."

The men looked at each other and shook their heads. Verl knew the thoughts in their minds. The picture had suddenly broadened. Before they were after two dynamiters of a railroad car. Now they wanted Cassidy and his bunch for a robbery and two murders.

"Where do you think they'd go?" Verl asked.

"I wish to God I knew," Welles said and scowled. "They'll be running hard now. Cassidy probably has some definite destination in mind." He beat a fist into a palm. "He could make a run for it all the way to the border. But I'm guessing he won't. He's made a big haul, and he'll want to hide until the furor dies down." He swore in frustration. "The only trouble is, that could be any of a hundred places."

"But you've got a guess," Verl persisted.

"I'd say Brown's Park or Robber's Roost. Either place could hide a small band for months. It's going to take considerable looking, whichever place he picks." He climbed back into his saddle and grinned painfully. "I'm like Sam. I was looking forward to a night of living like civilized men. Well, let's get going."

Verl dropped back and rode beside Travis. "Sorry things changed, Sam."

123

Travis' face contorted in sudden rage, and Verl wondered if the rage was at him.

"This is what I'm paid for," Travis growled. He rode with his eyes fixed ahead, his chin low.

Verl felt admiration for Travis. This was going to physically hurt the old man, but the thought of turning back was the furthest thing from his mind.

Verl thought about Kale and Kyle. They were digging the hole for themselves deeper, and, he thought grimly, already it was too deep for either of them to climb out.

Chapter Twenty

Brown's Park was located on the Utah-Colorado border just south of the Wyoming line. It was a thirty-mile-long valley along the Green River.

"It's got quite a history," Welles said as he sat his horse beside Verl's. "I guess William Ashley and his fur trappers were the first to look on this. The park is named after Baptiste Brown, one of the first settlers, if not the first. Peaceful-looking country, isn't it?"

"Beautiful," Verl said in appreciation.

"It was, until the outlaws took it over about 1860. They began by stealing horses and cattle from the wagon trains that were moving west. That was petty stuff compared to what came later. The big rustling came after the Civil War. Unemployed trail hands and other drifters took their toll of the big longhorn herds moving from Texas to Wyoming and Montana. Brown's Park was an ideal place to winter the stolen cattle until they could be sold."

Welles's face had a grim cast as he went on. "For too long, the fastest gun was the only law here. I can show you dozens of graves scattered along the river—men

124

who weren't as fast as they thought. A lot of their cabins still stand. Any one of those old, abandoned cabins could be Cassidy's pick for a hideout."

Verl blew out a deep breath. "This is a damned big place. Are we going to have to look over all of it?"

Welles grinned at Verl's agitation. "It's not as bad as it sounds. A few scattered ranchers live around here, and every now and then you run across an occasional store, struggling to hang on. Somebody is bound to see a bunch as big as Cassidy's. It's not hopeless."

The tedious search started. Welles went about it slowly and methodically. Verl investigated a dozen shacks, but not a one showed recent signs of being lived in. The dust was thick and unbroken on the floors, and the pack rats had been left undisturbed to assemble their treasures. He didn't see a single corral around any of the shacks, and remarked on it.

"A smart outlaw never built his corral near the shack," Welles explained. "An occupied corral was a sure sign somebody was there. No, a wise outlaw preferred to build his corral out of sight from his shack and walk back and forth to it. It was a lot safer that way."

"My God," Verl exploded. "We'll never get this job done. We've spent almost a full day already, and what have we accomplished?"

Welles was amused by Verl's lack of patience. "Losing your head and rushing things won't make it go a minute faster. We've accomplished one thing."

Verl's jaw jutted out. "Name it."

"We know that the corner of the park we've covered doesn't hold Cassidy and his bunch." He chuckled as Verl's belligerence didn't fade. "That's something, isn't it? Put enough of those corners together, and we've covered the park."

Verl frowned at him. Welles was unperturbed. He was taking this search a day at a time, and Verl admitted, grudgingly, that was probably the best way.

"I guess I'd have made a poor lawman," he grumbled. "Not enough patience."

Welles chuckled again. "I can tell you what it would have got you in a hurry. Dead."

He laughed uproariously at Verl's pained expression.

When he got his laughter under control, he pointed ahead of him. "Rundown ranch ahead. Somebody there. Smoke coming from the chimney. And the corral with horses in it is close to the house. That man isn't trying to hide from anybody."

An old man saw them coming before they arrived, for he was outside the house to greet them as they rode up.

"Howdy," he said and spit a spurt of tobacco through his long, stained beard. "Anything I can do for you gents?" There was no more warmth or friendliness in that than in his original greeting.

Welles hooked a knee over the horn. "I'm Dan Welles. This is a posse." He waved a hand at the men around him. "We're from the Pinkerton Detective Agency."

"I'm Priam Quigley," the old man returned. His cackle was mirthless. "I sure know you boys ain't looking for me. I ain't done anything wrong."

"That wasn't hard to guess," Welles said and smiled. "We're looking for Butch Cassidy and his bunch."

A shadow crossed Quigley's eyes. "Why?" he asked bluntly.

"They robbed a bank in Rock Springs. Killed two innocent men."

With the cloak of the beard, it was hard to tell whether or not emotion touched the old face. Verl thought, Maybe Quigley has no intention of talking. Cassidy had a reputation for being generous to small ranchers. Maybe, in the past, Cassidy had done small favors for this Quigley.

"The goddamned outlaws," Quigley said passionately. "This used to be God's land—until the outlaws moved in and changed everything." He spit again. "One of Cassidy's bunch killed a good friend of mine a couple of years back. I don't hold to no killings. And I sure don't hold to robbing another man." He squinted up at Welles. "You sure it was Cassidy?"

"I talked to eyewitnesses," Welles said patiently. "There's no doubt."

Quigley took a moment longer to make up his mind. "I guess that settles it, don't it? I saw the bunch you're after. Nine men and five women. They came by here and watered their horses. I thought it smartest to let them have their way without interfering. They were in one hell of a hurry. They didn't linger long. I'll admit their going eased me." He nodded slowly. "Yes, one of them was Cassidy. Recognized him from the window. I've seen him before."

Verl heard Welles's sigh of relief. They were still on the right trail. Welles was satisfied, but Verl had to learn more before he could know the same feeling.

"Mr. Quigley, did you happen to see two men who looked alike? In fact, they are twins."

"I think I did."

"How long ago did they leave?" Welles asked.

Quigley pondered over that for a moment. "A good two days ago, maybe three. Time has a way of slipping away from me." He pointed to the south. "That way. As I told you, they seemed to be in one big hurry."

"Thank you, sir," Welles said softly. "You've made our job easier." He touched his fingers to the brim of his hat and lifted his reins.

Verl spurred his horse to join Welles. Welles's face was alive with satisfaction. "I knew we'd run across somebody who'd caught a look at them."

"Does that mean we can forget about the rest of the park?" Verl asked.

"No, it doesn't," Welles said emphatically. "From what Quigley said, it looks like they've moved on. But we'd be damn fools to go on without checking out every possibility."

The posse spent three more days, looking through the park. Verl looked in twenty cabins that formerly belonged to outlaws. Welles seemed to know every outlaw who had ever lived in these cabins.

Verl looked at the dreary insides of one cabin and said thoughtfully, "Not much of a life, was it?"

"Not unless a man thoroughly enjoys living alone."

This was the kind of life Kale and Kyle had chosen, wanted and harried until a peaceful night's sleep was a rare thing.

Verl shrugged. It was what they wanted. He felt no pity for them.

Welles looked back down the line of riders. "How do you think Sam is doing, Verl? I thought he hobbled more at breakfast this morning."

"He did," Verl stated. "This trip is really beginning to pull at him. I wish to God he'd turn back."

"Why don't you suggest it to him?"

Verl grimaced. "And get thoroughly cussed out. Why don't *you* do it? You're the boss man."

Welles shrugged. "For the same reason you don't. Sam's got a rough tongue. His pride couldn't stand the thought that he couldn't keep up."

Verl nodded soberly. You could abuse a man's body, but you couldn't touch his pride.

Chapter Twenty-one

They rode through the dry, desolate Nine Mile Canyon, and the days mingled into one gray stretch of time after another. Food was tasteless, and sleep, at best, was fitful and troubled. Verl lay awake for long stretches at a time, thinking of how men drove themselves—each with varied reasons, but the results were the same. It only increased his hatred of Kale.

Welles stopped on a hill overlooking as miserable a country as Verl had ever seen. "That's it," Welles said, waving an expansive hand over the landscape below him. "Robber's Roost. The last of the three big stopping points along the outlaw trail."

"It looks like the gateway to hell," Verl commented.

"As close as a man wants to get," Welles agreed. He looked broodingly out over the formidable expanse of tortured land. It was laced through by rugged, twisting canyons. Within a few miles beyond the entrance, a man could be hopelessly lost unless he knew the country. It was parched land, rarely broken by green, growing things.

Verl looked at the foreboding land. "Seems almost hopeless," he said slowly.

"Yep," Welles agreed. "There's lookout points on every side. The outlaws live in sandstone caves or in crude cabins. The minute we ride in there, we'll be under surveillance. Maybe Cassidy already knows we're here."

"How do you know he's here?" Verl asked in a sudden burst of irritation.

"Instinct, I guess. It's like a man knows a rattlesnake's around before he sees or hears the snake. I've got a crawling in my skin. The feeling grew stronger with every passing mile. I'll never feel it any stronger than I do now.

"Watch your step," Welles went on. "They won't give any advance notice. When we least suspect it, they'll cut down on us. That's enough reason why so few lawmen ever brought their man out of this place."

"A pleasant picture," Verl said sourly.

Welles grinned bleakly. "Isn't it?"

He stood in his stirrups, raised his arm and swept it forward. "We're going in," he called. "Keep your eyes open. If anybody gets careless, he won't live to remember it."

Verl saw the impossibility of the task ahead of them before they'd gone very deeply into the first canyon. The canyon closed about them, its sheer walls rising steeply so that only a narrow strip of the sky could be seen. Verl tried to scan the walls and watch the twisting trail behind him. Nobody spoke a word. An occasional thud of a hoof against a stone was the only sound. Verl knew what was happening to him, and it was happening to the others. A man's skin grew so tight that it was painful at the anticipation of a rifle barking out, its echoes slamming from wall to wall. His head swiveled as he tried to cover all directions. It couldn't be done, and his anger mounted.

Whatever a lawman was paid, it was too damned little, Verl thought grimly. He wondered how much additional stress already strained nerves could take before they snapped.

129

The little cavalcade stopped for the night at a spring. Verl took a mouthful of the water, then spat it out.

Welles grinned at Verl's expression. "Iron," he said. "It'll coat your insides, but it won't kill you."

Verl ran his tongue around his mouth, trying to rid himself of the unpleasant taste. "Dying of thirst couldn't be much worse than drinking this stuff."

"It won't take long to change your mind," Welles answered calmly. "Fill your canteen. It's a long ride to the next spring."

Swearing, Verl filled his canteen. Even the horses didn't like this unpalatable stuff.

The iron content in the water even made the food taste awful, or else Verl was too tired to eat much. My God, it was unbelievable that men would subject themselves to such punishment—one man, for the few dollars he stole; the other, trying to stop him.

The strained nerves were showing, for men ate silently. The former good-humored banter was entirely missing. Verl didn't try to talk to Travis, even though Travis was right beside him. Travis ate poorly, putting his plate down after a few bites. Travis sat there, his shoulders slumped, his eyes hollowed and red-rimmed. With the growth of beard on that cavernous face, he looked like a caricature of a human being.

The men were more animated the next morning, and they ate with better appetites. "Dan," one of them said, "I believe you called this one wrong. They're not in here. I'm guessing, by now they're well on their way to Mexico."

Welles' face was set hard. "Don't bet on that," he said. "I know most of you don't agree with me. But don't let your caution ease off because of that. I think you'll get proof they're in here before the day is out."

Proof that Welles was right came before the morning was out. There was no sound, no indication that everything wasn't right, but a rifle shot rang out. The man riding third in line made no outcry. He just threw up his arms and pitched out of the saddle. His frightened horse bolted down the canyon and barely squeezed by the horses before him.

Verl got a confused impression of eyes going round and startled in taut faces. The men had no time to just sit and wonder, for their horses started plunging and bucking.

"Dismount," Welles yelled. "Lead your horses over against the base of the canyon wall." He set an example by jumping off, then tugging on the reins and hurrying up against the wall on the left side.

Verl heard harsh, labored breathing as the other men followed suit. They cowered against the rocky wall, their lips compressed in a thin line.

"Where did that come from?" somebody called.

Verl hadn't seen a thing, and he had been watching carefully.

"It came from up above," Welles replied. "I caught a glimpse of a wisp of smoke. I couldn't be sure before the breeze swept it away."

He stared frozenly at the limp, inanimate form on the canyon floor. "Poor Jeff. He never knew what hit him." He shook his head and sighed. "I guess if it's got to come, that's the best way."

"Any way of getting up there?" Verl asked.

Welles decisively shook his head. "If we could climb this wall, the ambusher would be long gone before we got to the top. I think it was only a warning to turn back. Next time, the warning won't be so gentle."

"What are we going to do about Jeff?" Verl asked.

"We'll see if we can wait out that backshooter," Welles said. A little heat crept into his voice. "You didn't think I was going off and leave Jeff there, did you?"

A good three hours passed before Welles said to his men: "I think we've outwaited him. Dash across the canyon to the opposite wall. That might give you a view of the top. If that killer's still there, maybe you can force him to lay low."

Welles and Verl remained behind. As the last man crossed without drawing fire, Welles said: "He's gone. He only wanted to show us what lay ahead if we insisted on pushing on. Will you give me a hand, Verl?"

"Sure," Verl replied gruffly.

Welles went through the dead man's pockets and

pulled out a small sum of money and a couple of letters. His face was sober as he looked at them. "I've got to get these back to Nancy, his wife. They weren't married very long. They had a two-year-old son." He swore suddenly in an excess of passion.

Verl looked helplessly about him. Where were they going to find enough dirt or sand to bury Jeff?

Welles read the helpless expression correctly. "We can't bury him," he said gloomily. "The best we can do is pile rocks on him. A hell of a way to say goodbye to a friend." His face twisted at some thought. He kicked savagely at a rock no bigger than his fist and sent it clattering down the canyon. "Nancy must never know how this ended."

They toiled in the increasing heat to pile large rocks upon the blanket-covered body. "Make them as big as you can carry," Welles said as the cairn grew.

The noonday sun was now pouring into the canyon, and sweat poured down Verl's face. The cairn was a good thirty inches tall before Welles finally stopped. He looked broodingly at the crude grave, then said, "I guess that's about as good as we can do." He broke into sudden impassioned swearing. "Oh goddamn it! Not even a decent marker to put on his grave."

"The men who rode with him won't need any marker to remember Jeff," Verl said quietly.

Welles nodded heavily. "I guess you're right," he muttered.

They walked together to rejoin the waiting men. "Think it can happen again?"

"I know it," Welles said emphatically. "Anyplace along this damned canyon. They've stated what they're going to do. We'll just have to be that much more cautious."

Verl allowed himself a strained grin. "At least nobody will argue with you again about the possibility of Cassidy and his bunch being here."

"A sorry consolation," Welles muttered. "I'd rather be proved wrong."

Chapter Twenty-two

Getting out of the canyon was a hellish trip. "I'm glad that's over," Verl said. At least the canyon didn't squeeze in on them. They could look around and see some open ground.

Welles gave him a harried glance. "We'll be in another one in less than twenty minutes. This area is laced with canyons, and they run in all directions."

"Will the second one be like the first?"

"Probably," Welles said dryly. "Cassidy now knows we're here. He also knows we have no intention of turning back. Now he'll do everything he can to change our minds."

"Oh Lord," Verl said softly.

"Now you're beginning to realize why lawmen dread the Robber's Roost," Welles said. "I can understand how the smart ones avoid this place. And nobody can call them cowards either."

Verl nodded. "I guess not." His sudden laugh had a brittle ring.

Welles pulled up and waited until the other horsemen gathered around him. "We're heading into another canyon. If anything, it's worse than the one we just left."

His words put the familiar tightness back into the watching faces.

"Ain't there some way to avoid it?" one of them asked.

Welles shook his head. "This is the only route in here that I know. Watch every foot of the canyon we cover. That includes both rims. Cassidy is as sly as a damned snake. You never know when or where he will strike."

Welles looked from face to face. "Anybody who

wants to pull out now can do so. I'll understand. There'll be no blame," he added softly.

Verl watched the play of emotions on the men's faces as they looked at each other. There was a desperate seeking for solidarity. Verl suspected that if any one of them accepted Welles' offer, it would be the signal for a concentrated exodus.

Bill Lafferty chewed off a bite of tobacco, worked it over thoroughly, then spat an amber stream at the ground. "None of us figured we'd be taking on Cassidy when we started." He chewed reflectively, his eyes veiled. "But if a man breaks loose now he'd probably never get back alone. Hell, Dan, you're the only one who knows his way around in this damned country. It looks like the only thing we can do is go on with you."

Heads around him bobbed, and Verl caught the reluctance in the gestures. They were caught in one sticky web: damned if they went on, and damned if they tried to pull back.

Verl saw the stiffness ebb out of Welles's face. He hadn't realized until then just how tight Welles had been. Welles hadn't known which way the men would go.

"Then, we go ahead," Welles said crisply. "But for God's sake, keep your eyes open."

They moved slowly ahead, and the gloomy depths of the canyon engulfed them. They had an advantage they lacked before; this canyon was wider. Welles kept them in a double file, one against either side of the canyon. It gave one file meager protection, sparse shelter from the rim directly overhead, but the other file was open to fire from the opposite rim.

The attack came with brutal unexpectedness. Verl's first indication they were under fire was the blast of a shot, its echoes rocketing from one wall to the other.

Even with all their alertness, men were caught by surprise. They whirled their horses to face the direction from which the shot came, and they were caught in a withering crossfire.

All around Verl, men screamed as they were hit. The canyon reverberated with the unceasing roar of the rifles. Men frantically tried to locate the source of the attack, and no one was certain which direction to face.

Horses reared and plunged, their frightened screaming adding to the unholy din.

Verl saw a man go down, then another. He forced Jigger toward where he had last seen Welles.

Welles's face was rigid with shock and rage. "My God," he said huskily. "We're caught in a crossfire. We were watching the heights, and the shots came from about halfway up. I saw some rifle flashes from that sandstone cave." He pointed it out, and Verl looked at the mass of shadow that marked an opening some twenty feet over their heads.

He jerked his head to the other side and saw another shadowy mass.

Welles was hopelessly trapped; and, by his agonized expression, he knew it. Verl stilled Jigger's plunging and yelled, "What do we do, Dan?" He could see only one course: run for it.

Welles started to reply, and his face went rigid with shock.

Verl knew he was bad hit. He saw that he was too late to reach Welles. Welles's eyes were wide and staring, but he tried to retain his balance in the saddle. A gush of blood poured from his mouth, and he pitched to the ground.

The horrible limpness with which Welles fell told Verl that Welles was mortally hit. Still, he might have hesitated, seeking some futile hope of getting out of this trap.

Then he saw Travis slump in the saddle. Only a frantic grip at the horn saved him from falling. Verl spurred beside Travis and leaned out to extend an arm to assist him.

"Hang on, Sam. We're getting out of here."

Their progress was agonizingly slow, for Verl couldn't risk a run that might tear Travis from his hand and out of the saddle. Every step of the way, angry little bees sought them out. Verl flinched each time he heard their hum, for those bees carried a fatal sting.

"We're not going to make it," Verl thought frantically. On both sides of him, men spurred desperately to outrun the bullets. They soon outdistanced Verl and

Travis, and Verl thought dully, the bastards are leaving us. He gave that thought some consideration. In their place, maybe he would have done the same thing. But he had to get Travis out of this.

He couldn't believe his ears. Surely his hearing was tricking him, but he no longer heard the passage of rifle slugs, or the reports of guns. He could draw an unharried breath. He could almost believe they had made it out of the canyon.

They came out into the relatively open ground between the two canyons. Travis was in bad shape. His breathing wheezed through his open mouth, and his color was horrible.

"Hold on, Sam," Verl begged. "Just a little farther." Ahead of him he saw the other men. They had stopped when the danger lessened.

Verl rode up to them. He jumped off to assist Travis from his horse, and Travis' weight almost crushed him to the ground.

"You're going to be all right now, Sam." Even as Verl said it, he saw there was no basis for relief over Travis' condition.

He lowered Travis to the ground and straightened him out. "Wait until I get my canteen, Sam. Then we'll see how bad it is."

"Won't do any good, Verl." Travis went into a paroxysm of coughing, and his lips were bloodstained after the effort.

He looked up at Verl through pain-hazed eyes. "Maybe things would have turned out differently, Verl, if you'd told me about Kale and Kyle right at the start."

Verl flinched at the reproach in Travis' voice. Before he could say anything, Travis coughed again. He looked too weary to keep his eyes open. The light went out of them, and Verl knew Travis was dead.

He had never known such terrible rage. It rocked and shook him. He had a wild impulse to go back and find Kale and Kyle. Then the blinding moment of fury passed, and he realized how foolish that would be.

The men were gathered around him, and Verl raised his head.

"What are we going to do now?" one of them asked.

136

For an instant that insanity returned, and Verl replied. "We could go back in after them." They had left three good men back there, and another out here.

The man shook his head. "Not me." He looked at the others, and they slowly nodded agreement. The speaker's face turned more aggressive. "Why, goddamn it," he exploded, "nine of us rode in there. You know how many came out. What are you trying to do? Get all of us killed? *My* car wasn't dynamited. It's the damned railroad's car. Let *them* do something about it." He searched for a clinching argument. "Welles is dead. I saw him fall. He's the only one who even began to know something about this country. What do you want us to do, stumble around blind?"

The man made sense, and Verl said dully, "No, of course not."

"Then, let's get out of here."

Verl shook his head. "I'm not leaving until I see that Travis has some kind of burial."

"Let's get it done, then," the man said and swung down.

This was the second cairn Verl had helped to build. He kept the men busy piling rock on Travis' body until he was satisfied.

"I guess that does it," he said wearily. Still, he stood there a long moment, trying to think of something to say. I'm sorry, Sam, he thought, and let it go at that. He hoped Sam would understand.

He swung up and headed for the opening of the first canyon. A man riding beside him groaned, "We have to go through that damned thing again? God, what if they're waiting for us?"

"I don't think they are," Verl replied. He wished he could be more convincing. But maybe Cassidy would be satisfied. Hadn't he kicked the hell out of them? He had seen them run. That should satisfy him. But just the same, Verl wouldn't be completely easy until he rode out of Robber's Roost.

Chapter Twenty-three

Verl would never forget that return trip, if he lived to be a hundred. Men spoke to each other only if absolutely necessary. They sat around the evening campfire, their eyes remote. Actually, they looked at nothing, unless it was the galling remembrance of their failure. These men were weary of spirit, and it was far more telling than any physical fatigue.

Verl left the little group just outside of South Pass. He wanted to get home as quickly as possible. Jabez would be waiting anxiously for his report.

He rode into the yard, and Jabez was outside, talking to Carl Anderson. The house looked the same as ever, perhaps a little more dreary.

Carl saw him first. Astonishment spread over his face, and he cried, "Why, it's Verl."

Jabez whirled and limped over to where Jigger stood. His face shone with eagerness. "You been gone a long time, son."

"Long enough," Verl said tersely. "Things go all right here?"

Jabez sensed the guardedness in Verl's manner. Verl didn't want to talk about what had happened, not with an outsider present.

"Things went fine," Jabez said stoutly. "Carl's a good hand." He tried to smile at Verl, but the attempt didn't quite come off. "If Tom's agreeable, I might talk to him about trading you for Carl."

The sense of failure still rode heavily on Verl. "Could be a smart idea, Pa," he said soberly.

Jabez stared at him. Something had happened to change Verl, something bad. "That was just a poor joke," Jabez said contritely. "You know I didn't mean—"

"Forget it, Pa," Verl said wearily. "I've got to take care of Jigger. He's plumb worn out."

"Sure, son. Anything we can do to help?"

Verl shook his head. At the moment, he wanted to be alone to sort out his thoughts. He had to find the right words to tell Jabez what had happened. There was no easy way, he concluded.

He swung down and, leading Jigger to the barn, stopped long enough to shake hands with Carl. "Appreciate what you did, Carl, though that's pretty poor pay. Maybe I can make it up to you someday."

"You ain't beholden to me for anything," Carl said stoutly. "If we got in a jam, you'd give us a hand, wouldn't you?"

"You know it." Verl never meant anything more.

He led Jigger into the barn, stripped the saddle, blanket, and bridle from him. He put them in their proper place, then poured out a generous portion of oats into Jigger's manger. He picked up a curry brush and went to work. Lord, Jigger needed this cleaning. Between strokes, Verl listened to Jigger's greedy eating.

"Been on scanty rations, haven't you, boy?" he murmured. "Things will be different from now on." He'd see to that, but it was going to take time before the gloss returned to Jigger's coat.

Verl finished currying Jigger and left the barn. He walked into the house, and Jabez was seated at the kitchen table. "I've got coffee made." Jabez was concerned. Verl looked like hell.

"I could use it," Verl grunted. He shook his head at the offer of food. "Not now, Pa. Maybe I'll feel more like eating a little later." Right now, just the effort of eating seemed too great.

Jabez put his concern into words. "Verl, you look like hell."

"I ought to," Verl said with no rancor. "I've been through it." His eyes were frozen as he relived those few terrible minutes when death reached out for all of them.

"You don't have to talk about it if you don't want to," Jabez said softly.

139

Verl gave him a bleak smile. "Maybe talking about it will get it off my mind. Pa, we got the hell kicked out of us. Ten men rode into Robber's Roost. Worst damned piece of land I ever laid eyes on. One canyon after another. Men can easily get lost there." He was silent, his eyes brooding. "Ten men rode into those canyons, Pa. Five rode out. We ran into an ambush Butch Cassidy and his bunch laid."

Jabez's eyes went round in surprise. "Why did he cut down on you?"

"That bunch robbed a bank and killed two men in Rock Springs. I'm pretty sure the twins were in on that too."

"Did you see them?" Jabez asked, his voice brittle.

Verl briefly closed his eyes. "I didn't get a smell of them. But I know they were with Cassidy. Travis and the Pinkertons were after the twins. After the bank robbery they switched their attention to Cassidy."

He paused a moment. He was going to have to tell Jabez about Travis, and that would hurt him.

"It was a hell of a trip on Sam," he went on in a tired voice. "I saw him going down daily." He drew a deep breath. "He didn't come out, Jabez." There, it was said.

Jabez looked like he'd been kicked in the stomach. He beat an impotent fist on the table.

Verl nodded. "We buried him the best we could, Pa. We left some men just lying there. There was no way we could get to them."

"Goddamn those twins," Jabez said bitterly. "They started all this. I hold them responsible for Sam's death."

Verl shrugged. So did he, but he couldn't see where that was going to do any good.

"I guess they go scot free." The bitterness was more pronounced in Jabez's voice.

"No," Verl said flatly.

"You're not thinking of going after them again," Jabez protested.

"No," Verl said quietly. "An army couldn't accomplish that." He looked at the racking anguish in Jabez's face and cried: "How do you think *I* feel? I carried Owen's rifle, and I didn't get a single chance to use it."

They sat in silence, each wrapped in his own bitter thoughts.

Jabez broke the silence by saying: "Nobody's blaming you, Verl. You did all you could. But it goes down hard to think of Kale and Kyle going unpunished for what they did."

"They won't be," Verl promised. "All the way back I thought about it. I found out nobody can go in to Robber's Roost and bring them out. But maybe there's a way to draw them out. Make them come to us."

Jabez was shaking his head in objection. "How are you going to do that? They won't leave a safe hiding place."

"I don't know yet, Pa. But there's got to be a way. It'll come to me."

He stood abruptly and said, "Pa, I'm going to bed. Maybe a night's sleep will clear my head."

"Sure." Jabez's tone said he thought Verl's promise a flimsy thing.

Verl looked back from the door. Jabez still sat there, his shoulders slumped.

Chapter Twenty-four

"You'll eat some breakfast, won't you, Verl?" Jabez said as Verl came into the kitchen in the morning.

"I can eat this morning," Verl said gently. He had thought about what he could do most of the night, and nothing came to him. "I've got to go into South Pass this morning. Ann and Cleatis will be anxious to hear about Etta."

"She's still with Kale?"

"The last I heard, she was. It's going to be hard to tell them."

"Let it go, Verl."

Verl knew Jabez was talking about the whole matter, just forget about Kale and Kyle as though they had never existed. He pressed his father's shoulder. "I can't forget it, Pa, but I won't do anything foolish." He had tried that once, and it hadn't worked. Maybe he had gone at it from the wrong end. "Good breakfast, Pa."

"Verl, you're not riding off again, are you?" Jabez begged.

"No long trip this time," Verl promised. "I'll be around."

He went out the door and headed toward the barn. In the days he had been gone, spring had definitely arrived. The air was almost soft. Too balmy for a sheepskin, he thought absently. But he didn't go back into the house to take off the heavy coat.

"More work for you, Jigger," he said.

Jigger nickered eagerly. He seemed eager to go. A night's rest had done him a world of good.

Verl saddled and mounted. It did you more good than it did me, Verl thought as he headed for South Pass. His face was frozen, but thoughts kept bubbling up in his mind. The only trouble was that he couldn't find anything solid to get hold of.

Damn you, Kale, he thought wearily. I'm not giving up. All his life Kale had been determined to have things his way. So far, nothing had changed that. But there should be a way to turn things around, and Verl's mind went back to work on the problem. If Kale had a solid admirable trait, it was that dogged determination. The only trouble was that it was applied to the wrong things. Verl almost smiled as he recalled the dogged purpose Kale had displayed in searching for Indian Charley's gold mine. Kale believed the mine existed, and he hadn't let go until after several years of trailing and searching.

Verl's eyes widened, and he straightened in the saddle. An idea was beginning to form. He didn't know whether or not it was plausible, but it just *could* work. That mine had a tremendous fascination for Kale. Enough to pull him out of Robber's Roost? Verl didn't know, but this might be worth thinking about.

He rode through South Pass City and stopped before

the Fabers' house. Ann must have seen him coming, for she opened the door before he reached the porch. She flew toward him, her arms outstretched, her face radiant.

"Oh, Verl," she cried as she hugged him. "I've been so worried. You were gone so long." She plastered his face with kisses, then pressed her lips against his.

She was the one to break away. "I'm sorry, Verl," she whispered. "Somebody might pass by and see us."

"Let 'em," he retorted and pulled her closer.

It was Verl who raised his head. "I came to tell you and Cleatis what happened."

The grimness of his tone made her search his face. "It was bad, wasn't it?" she asked quietly.

"I just hope to God I never have to go through something like that again." He started to add more, and Ann pressed her fingers against his lips. "Not now, Verl. Wait until Cleatis can hear it too."

He nodded his agreement and followed her into the house.

Cleatis was slumped in a chair in the parlor, and Verl saw the hollowed eyes, the sunken cheeks. My God, how this has aged him, he thought. He looked quickly about the room, and the shadows returned to his eyes. This was where Owen had died.

Cleatis shook Verl's hand, and his grip was flaccid. Those haunted eyes searched Verl's face, and Cleatis made his own summary. "It was a bad trip," he stated.

Verl grimaced. "That's understating it."

Cleatis' sigh seemed to come from his bowels. "I was hoping you'd come back with Etta. She meant a lot to me."

"Five men lost their lives on that trip," Verl said harshly. "Kale and Kyle joined up with Cassidy's bunch. It looks like Etta chose to go with them. On their run to Robber's Roost, they robbed a bank in Rock Springs. Two more men died in that holdup." Verl beat his hands together. "We tried, Cleatis, but we ran into an ambush. Cassidy knew that country too well."

The jubilation at seeing Ann was gone, and Verl sank into a chair. "Nobody could have brought them out."

143

"I'm not criticizing you," Cleatis defended himself. "You did everything you could. But I so hoped you'd bring Etta back," he mourned.

Verl wearily shook his head. "Nothing will change as long as they remain in Robber's Roost. The only way anybody can get at them is if they decide to come out."

"What good would that do?" Cleatis asked dejectedly. "We won't know when they leave, or which direction they'll take. I don't see where that'd be any help at all."

Verl leaned forward, his face more intense. "I've been thinking about that all the way here. What if we could come up with an idea that would pull Kale and Etta out of Robber's Roost? What if we know exactly where they'll be heading?"

Cleatis looked at him, startled, then said: "It'd take something pretty big to do that. I don't see what it could be."

"Ever since Kale was a kid, he's been fascinated by wealth. I remember he spent most of three years trying to track down Indian Charley's mine."

Cleatis snorted with more vigor. "Everybody knew there was nothing to that. Just a story that grew."

Verl nodded. "Yes, but Kale didn't know that. Many an evening I listened to him talk about what he would do when he found all that gold."

Cleatis was not impressed. "He was just a kid then. He's probably forgotten all about it now."

"I just wonder," Verl mused. "If we could put out bait attractive enough, it might draw Kale back. That idea of being wealthy was stuck pretty hard in his head."

Cleatis was interested in spite of his doubt. "Just what would that bait be?"

"Suppose I found that mine and spread the news around town. It might get back to Kale."

"Who would believe it enough to carry the story back to Kale?"

"That's my problem right now. If I had some nuggets to show around and claim they came from Indian Charley's mine, that might just do it. Particularly if Kale hears *I* found it. That would gall him good." Verl's face lengthened. "But I'd need some nuggets to show around, and I don't even know where to begin looking for them. Gold played out in this country a long time back. I don't know anybody around who even has any."

Cleatis pulled at his lower lip, wrestling with a decision. "I may have what you need. I'll be right back." He grunted with the effort it took to stand, and left the room.

"Do you think it will work, Verl?" Ann asked. "If it only could. Did you see Cleatis' face. It came alive. You put new hope in him."

"It may not work," Verl said honestly. "There's so many strings to tie together. I'm not even sure how I could get the news that I found the mine to Kale. And I don't know if the old fascination still has its former hold. It's the best thing I could come up with. The *only* thing."

He stared at the floor until Cleatis returned. Oh, he could pick so many flaws in this plan. But when a man is desperate for shelter in stormy weather, he picks any roof he can find.

Cleatis came back into the room, carrying a small, buckskin bag. He unfastened the drawstrings and said, "Hold out your hand, Verl."

Verl held out his hand, and Cleatis poured out a small cascade of nuggets. He had seen gold nuggets before, enough to recognize the dull golden shine.

"Cleatis, where did you get these?"

"They're from my mining days. I kept this small bag in memory of better times. Besides, they could come in handy if a man got short of cash." His voice had a livelier note. "Just getting this little bag out reminded me of the fascination I once knew. It could be the same with Kale."

Cleatis' enthusiasm could be carrying him too far, and the ultimate result could be only another bitter disappointment. Verl had to warn him. "Cleatis, this might not work at all. Even if it does, it'll take time for the news to get back to Kale, and more time to draw him back. At best, there'll be a long wait."

"I don't give a damn how long it takes," Cleatis said violently. "I only want Etta back." His face was suddenly anxious. "Do you think she'll come back with him?"

"I think you can bet on it," Verl said calmly. "Can I take these with me? I'm not promising I'll be able to return them."

"I'd give anything to see this work." A thought occurred to Cleatis, for his eyes clouded. "With this small amount, it's going to be hard to convince anybody of a big strike."

"Not if I bring sacks of rocks into town and claim they're full of nuggets," Verl said. He was beginning to feel a new rush of excitement racing through him. "I'm going down and talk to Evans at the bank. I'll need his help."

Cleatis nodded decisively. "You can trust old John. I think he hates a lawbreaker as much as anybody."

He walked with Ann and Verl to the door. "You'll let us know what happens, Verl?" he asked wistfully.

"That's another sure bet you can make," Verl replied. He put on his hat, bent and brushed Ann's cheek with his lips. "I'll be in touch with you."

He looked back after he had mounted. Ann lifted a hand to wave at him, and Verl responded with a return wave. This was going to work. He knew it.

Chapter Twenty-five

John Evans sat behind a thoroughly beat-up desk. It should be; it had seen a lot of service. It had been used by Evans' father, and after John Evans had taken over, he hadn't seen any practical reason to buy new, fancy furniture. The conservative customers thought that was an admirable trait in a bank president.

Verl would guess Evans to be somewhere in his mid-fifties. He was getting plump, and Verl supposed that his indoor work was the culprit. Usually that round face was beaming with goodwill, but today the face was solemn, the eyes grave.

He stood as Verl reached his desk and extended a hand. "Heard about the results of your expedition, Verl. Some of the Pinkerton men stopped in town for a meal. God, I've never seen more beaten men. They didn't want to talk about it, but I pried a few words out of them. I'm telling you, those men will carry scars on their souls for the rest of their lives."

Verl sat down without being invited. "They will, John. Did you know Dan Welles?"

"Not well. I've talked to him a few times. I heard about him being killed. Damned shame. He was a good man."

"Travis got it too." Verl suspected Evans hadn't heard about that. He was right in his assumption, for Evans' face showed shock.

"Damn it, no," Evans protested. "I hate to hear that. Sam and I've been on a few fishing trips together." He stared at his hands lying loosely on the desk. "Sam was one hell of a fishing partner," he muttered. He raised his head and there was pain in his eyes. "Were Kale and Kyle responsible for this too?"

"A good part of it, John," Verl said matter-of-factly. Rapidly, he told of Kale and Kyle joining up with Cassidy, of the bank robbery in Rock Springs, and the death of two men there.

Evans kept shaking his head as though he couldn't believe it. "My God, Verl, the bill those two have run up. I remember them when they weren't two feet tall. Who would have thought they would turn out like this?"

"None of us," Verl said. "I didn't get them this time. But I'm not going to let it stop there."

Verl's words put a startled flash in Evans' eyes. "You're not thinking of going after them again?" he protested.

Verl grimaced. "No. All of that was knocked out of me. But if there was some way I could get them to come out where I could get at them—" His words trailed off, and his eyes were far away.

147

Evans knew Verl Wakeman well. "You've got something in mind?"

"Maybe just a wild hair," Verl confessed. "But it has a chance of working. Do you remember the time when Kale and Kyle were interested in Indian Charley's mine?"

In spite of the gravity of the conversation, Evans chuckled. "Everybody in town will remember that. I never saw two kids so caught up in an idea."

"What if they heard I found that mine?" Verl asked slowly. "Would that bring them back?"

Evans' jaw sagged before he recovered. "They wouldn't believe it," he stated firmly.

"They might, if the bait's made attractive enough." Verl pulled the small buckskin bag out of his pocket, opened the drawstrings, and dumped the nuggets out before Evans.

Evans fingered over the nuggets. Two of them were fair-sized. "Lord, how long has it been since I've seen something like this?" He raised his eyes and stared at Verl. "Where did you get them?"

"Cleatis gave them to me. He wants Etta back as bad as I want Kale."

Evans shook his head. "Not enough to convince anybody that you found that supposed mine. Besides, how would you get the news to Kale?"

"I need your help for that, John. I want to borrow some of the bank's money sacks. If I brought them back filled with rocks, wouldn't that go a long way toward making people believe?"

Evans got what he was driving at, for his eyes gleamed. "It could. It doesn't take much to stir people's imagination. But I still don't see how you'd get the news to Kale."

"I'll spread the news around town," Verl said calmly. "There's still quite a few shady characters here. One of them might try to take the news to Cassidy's bunch." He reached out and picked out the biggest nuggets. "I'll need these to show around. You hold the others. If anybody comes in to ask about them, you can show what I'm leaving you."

Evans whistled softly. "It just might work," he said

148

slowly. "You can have all the sacks you want. But it'll take a long time before you even know if it's working."

Verl nodded. "I've thought of that too, John. I'll be on watch. I can't involve anyone else in this. It could turn violent."

Evans got up from his desk, walked to a cabinet, and opened it. He came back with a thick pile of sacks. "This be enough?"

Verl grinned. "Should be. I'll be back in later today with some of them filled." He tucked the sacks under his coat. "You don't know how much I appreciate this."

"If anybody comes in to ask about this new strike, I'll do my part," Evans promised.

"I know you will." Verl shook Evans' hand. "If it works at all, you should be getting inquiries in two or three days. I don't have to tell you this is between you and me."

"You can count on me," Evans said. He walked with Verl to the door. "You just watch yourself, Verl. I don't know how big a hornet's nest you're stirring up."

Verl's teeth bared in a mirthless grin. "It could bring back Cassidy and his entire bunch. But somehow I doubt it. Cassidy doesn't have the crazy belief that the twins had. No, I think Cassidy will stay right where he is. He knows it won't be safe to come out for some time, after the mess he stirred up."

Evans slapped him on the shoulder. "Good luck, Verl."

Verl nodded soberly. "I'll need it."

He walked outside, climbed into the saddle and headed for home. He needed a few rocks with which to fill some of those sacks. And Jabez would be waiting anxiously to hear how things were going.

It was midafternoon when Verl returned to town. He had a half-dozen sacks, filled with rocks, tied behind his saddle. He made no effort to hide them. He wanted people to know.

He walked into the bank, carrying the sacks. Inside Evans' office, he laid them on the desk. "If that was gold, it'd draw a lot of hungry flies, wouldn't it?"

Evans hefted one of the sacks. "I'd be tempted to

149

turn crooked, if I thought these sacks contained gold."

Verl smiled. "If it would do that to you, John, think of what it would do to a less honest man. Going out to do a little drinking now. Want to spread the news of my good fortune around."

"I hope to God it gets results," Evans said fervently.

Verl put some thought on his selection of a saloon. He decided Branson's would be the most profitable. The big names of the outlaw world, plus the hangers-on of the criminal fringe hung out in Branson's.

He walked into the dingy room, and less than a half-dozen men were there. That suited him fine. It should insure him drawing attention.

The light was poor, and the paint was peeling off the walls. Verl couldn't even begin to guess at how long ago the sawdust on the floor had been changed.

Cold, reserved eyes swung to Verl at his entrance. Cassidy used to hang out here, but he was gone. Nobody here approached Cassidy's status, but any of these men could do what Verl wanted to accomplish.

He knew two or three of the men by sight. They gave him no greeting, and he offered none.

Verl walked up to the bar and nodded to the dumpy man behind it. No emotion moved Branson's fat face as he watched Verl. His eyes were a cold slate-gray.

"What'll it be?" Branson asked. There wasn't actual hostility in his voice, more of a guarded waiting. This place wasn't usually Verl's stomping ground.

"I'm celebrating the biggest thing in my life," Verl announced loudly. "I want the best whiskey in the house."

Branson nodded without comment, but curiosity was beginning to shine in his eyes. Verl didn't actually see heads turn toward him, but he had a feeling that everybody in the place was watching him.

Branson poured a shot glass and shoved it toward Verl. He started to withdraw the bottle, and Verl said in that same loud voice: "Leave it there. I can buy every bottle you have in the place." He laughed loudly. "Hell, I can buy the whole place."

That irritated Branson, for a dull flush stained his cheeks. "Big talk, mister," he said testily.

"You think I can't back it up? What do you think this is?" Verl pulled the small bag from his pocket and unloosened the drawstrings. A cascade of small gold nuggets tumbled out onto the bar.

Branson's breath came faster as he turned the nuggets over with a finger. "I'll be damned," he said hoarsely.

"Take what you need out of that," Verl said carelessly. "I've got plenty more."

"Haven't seen any gold in here for years." Branson's voice was brittle. "Where did you get this?"

The magic word "gold" pulled everyone to his feet, for Verl heard the scrape of chair legs and the scuff of feet.

"Wouldn't you like to know?" Verl asked scornfully.

That pinched Branson, for he snapped, "I'm not set up to handle gold. Take it back. I want cash."

Verl reached for the nuggets. "I've got that too."

Men were crowding about him now, and one of them asked, "Mind if we take a look at those, mister?"

"Help yourself," Verl invited. He knew the tall, slim man the best. This was Hamp Edison. There was talk that he had once ridden with Cassidy, though the last couple of years he wasn't seen around with Cassidy much. Some speculated there was an argument that had broken them up, though no one could be sure.

"My God," Edison said in an awed voice. He turned over the nuggets with a forefinger. "You got more of this stuff, mister?"

"I brought in six sacks filled with the same stuff. Took it to the bank today." Verl made no effort to disguise the bragging note in his voice. "And I've only begun."

Edison's eyes were narrow, calculating slits.

Verl would have given anything to know what was running through the man's mind. "You don't believe me?"

"Hard to believe," Edison murmured. "Hasn't been any gold in this country for years."

151

"They just quit looking in the right place," Verl said. "I'll stand for a round of drinks."

They accepted that, though that wasn't what they wanted. They wanted to hear more about this gold.

Verl raised his refilled glass to all of them. "I know the gold's supposed to be played out. A few people didn't believe it. Indian Charley didn't."

He clamped his lips tight, as though inadvertently he had let out something he hadn't wanted to say. He had sowed his first seeds. Now it was going to take torturous waiting to see if any of them came up.

"Well, I've got to get back to work," he said and winked at them. "Got to get back to the business of getting rich." He walked out of the saloon without looking back, but he'd bet he would be the sole subject of conversation the rest of the afternoon.

Chapter Twenty-six

Edison sauntered up to the teller's cage and asked, "Can I talk to the boss?"

"You mean Mr. Evans?"

Edison frowned at him. "Is he the big man here?" At the teller's nod, Edison said, "Then, Evans is the one I want to see."

"I'll have to have your name." The teller didn't flinch under those angry eyes. "I have to tell him who's calling, don't I?"

"All right," Edison growled. "Tell him it's Hamp Edison. I need some information from him."

The teller was gone only a few seconds. He came back and said, "Mr. Evans will see you."

"Good," Edison barked. He walked to the door, not sure of just what he would say. Evans might not be willing to tell him a damned thing.

He knocked at the door and entered at the "Come in."

Evans sat behind his desk, his face bland. "What can I do for you, Mr. Edison?" He waved at a chair. "Sit down."

Edison sat on the edge of the chair, running his hat around in his hands.

"Is it true there's been a big gold strike?" he blurted out.

"I don't know if you'd call it a strike or not, but there's certainly been some gold found. I'd say in rather astonishing quantities."

"I saw some nuggets," Edison muttered. "I thought the man was stringing us along."

Evans smiled brightly. "You must mean Verl Wakeman." He opened the drawer of his desk and fished out several nuggets. He leaned forward to place them before Edison. "Are these like the nuggets you saw? Verl left these with me."

Edison stared at them with bulging eyes. He could feel the throb beginning in his temples. "Is this stuff real?" he asked hoarsely.

"As real as any I've ever seen. My God, he must have a mountain of the stuff. He's brought in a dozen bags already, and he claims he's only begun."

Edison swallowed hard. "I saw him bring in a half-dozen sacks only a few minutes ago. So everything he said was for real?"

Evans nodded solemnly. "You can count on it."

"Did he say where he found the stuff?"

"If I knew, I wouldn't tell you. That's a confidential matter between the bank and its customer."

Edison ran his finger around the inside of his collar. "Don't seem right," he complained. "For one man to strike it rich and everybody else is cut out."

Evans leaned forward, and his attitude was conspiratorial. "I'll give you a guess, but you've got to remember it's only my guess. I think that gold came out of Indian Charley's mine. The one that everybody thought was lost for good." He nodded solemnly. "Well, I think Verl found it."

"Naw," Edison disclaimed. "That was just a story.

153

People looked for that mine pretty hard. They never found anything."

Evans nodded. "That's why I'm telling you Verl found it. I know his family has been fascinated with the subject for a long time. Did you know the twins, Kale and Kyle?"

Edison frowned. "I think I heard of them."

"I know from personal knowledge the twins hunted two or three years for Indian Charley's gold. They got in trouble and had to run for it. I heard they rode off with Cassidy."

He shrugged, dismissing the twins. "But Verl kept on looking for the mine. It looks like he won out." He frowned, as though something suddenly distressed him. "I've advised Verl to ship what gold he has, but he refuses. He wants to keep it intact until he takes all the gold there is." Evans smiled frostily. "Verl says he wants to be rich all at once. I can appreciate his feeling, but I still say it's foolhardy." He stood, indicating the conversation was terminated. "Now, if you'll excuse me, Mr. Edison, I've got to get back to bank business."

Edison hated to leave. His head reeled from facts and partial facts Evans had told him. He didn't know where that gold came from, but he was certain of one thing. There was a fortune in gold in the bank's vault. From what Evans just said, it would remain there for some time.

"Thanks," he mumbled and started for the door.

"Sorry I couldn't be of more help," Evans called after him.

He sat down after Edison left, and his smile was sly with the satisfaction of a predatory animal who had smelled and sighted its prey. Oh, he had lots to tell Verl when he next saw him.

Verl came in a day later, and his eyes were anxious. "Edison left town a couple of hours ago, John. He bought supplies that looked like he was going to be gone several days. He seemed in one hell of a hurry. Did he take the bait?"

"Hook, line, and sinker," Evans replied. He chuckled and related the conversation with Edison. "He believed every word I told him. I could see the wheels spinning around in his head. He thinks you're trying to amass a fortune before you cash it in. That was my own invention, Verl," he said modestly.

Verl rubbed his hands. "Good, good." He squinted reflectively across the room. "I don't know how well Edison knows Kale and Kyle, but I'd say he's on his way to tell Cassidy about this. Either way, Kale will hear about it too."

"What if Cassidy decides to come back and look into this?"

"If he and his bunch do come, it could make things a little sticky." His voice picked up a new bite. "I just don't believe he will. I think only Kale and Kyle will come back, maybe accompanied by Edison. His greed's been whetted. I'll be waiting for them," he finished grimly.

Evans' face was heavy. "I hate to see you try to handle this alone. You could get some help—"

"No," Verl said firmly. "This is *my* business. I haven't got the right to pull anybody else into it." A grin softened his face. "I know you're thinking about the danger to me, and I appreciate it. But damn it, John, just living is dangerous. A man could step out into the street, trip on a half hidden rock, and fall and break his neck."

Evans sighed at the hopelessness of trying to convince Verl he was foolhardy.

"If it goes according to your plan, when do you figure on seeing them?"

Verl did some rapid calculating. "It's a long, hard ride both ways. Usually, I'd say a week going and a week coming back. But if Edison was in a hurry, he could whittle a little off that. The same way with Kale and Kyle. I make it six days both ways. In twelve days, I'll be watching for them. John, I want to get this off my mind."

"I know you do," Evans said softly.

"There's only one really hard thing about it all," Verl said absently.

"What's that, Verl?"

"The damned waiting," Verl said with passion.

155

"Watching the days drag by and wondering if they're coming, or if they saw through the whole idea." He shook his head. "You never know," he muttered. A man could surely torture himself with his self-doubts.

"I've got a feeling it's going to turn out exactly as you planned, Verl."

"I hope to God you're right," Verl said fervently.

Chapter Twenty-seven

Kale sweated profusely under the strengthening Utah sun. God, how he was growing to detest this country. Life with Cassidy was nothing like he had imagined it. What he was doing now was pure, unadulterated slavery, and the pay for it was just about as bad.

Cassidy and some of the others had slipped out of the Roost, made a quick raid, and come back with twenty stolen horses. For the last three days, Cassidy and all of them had been busy, changing brands and further breaking the horses. Some of those animals were pretty wild. Kale limped from a kick he had received yesterday, and he was sick and tired of this unending toil.

"Hold still, damn you," he roared, and hauled on one of the ropes restraining a hammer-headed, moon-eyed horse, plunging and rearing at the end of three ropes.

The horse lunged again, almost dragging Kale off his feet.

"Damn you," Kale yelled in fury. "I'll beat your head off."

The memory of the exhilaration of those moments while the bank robbery was in progress was only a bitter taste in his mouth now. That was living, and it was highly rewarding. Most of the time they had been here had been spent on a few horse races, a lot of drinking, and more card playing. Kale found out he wasn't much of a card player. His part of the proceeds of the robbery was almost gone. His share out of the sale of the stolen horses would be nothing compared to what he had received from the robbery.

The horse was finally wrestled to the ground. Its feet were tied, and Curry sat on its head, while Longabaugh and Kilpatrick set about altering the brand with a running iron.

Kale retrieved his rope and re-coiled it. Why, this was no better than what he had left at home. Etta was getting pretty unhappy about it too. She hadn't said much, but her sullenness grew daily. It showed in her lack of interest in Kale's lovemaking at night. She didn't actually say so, but her changed attitude was a direct accusation. Kale had promised her better than this.

Cassidy came over to Kale and said, "We'll move them into Colorado tomorrow or the day after."

"All this work for damned poor pay," Kale groused.

"Ah," Cassidy said in quick perceptiveness. "You don't think it's worthwhile?"

"Not when I think of that robbery in Rock Springs," Kale retorted defiantly. "We were in and out of there in a matter of a few minutes. And we had something to show for it."

The criticism stung Cassidy, for his eyes sharpened. "Did you think it would be all gravy, Kale?" Cassidy's tone was almost mild. "It can't be like that robbery every day. Right now, we've got to sit tight until the heat dies down. Only then will we start thinking of another job."

Kale stared at the ground. He didn't dare let Cassidy see the rebellion burning in his eyes.

"We run things *my* way," Cassidy snapped. "Do you think it's smart to lay around, doing nothing? This way keeps everybody busy, and we make a few dollars." His tone picked up a bite. "If you don't like it, Kale, you can pull out."

That frightened Kale. If he did what Cassidy proposed, he would be practically on his own. Without the security of Cassidy's men around him and the protection of the Roost, he would be vulnerable.

157

"You've got to admit this is pretty wearing, Butch," he said feebly.

"Not to me," Cassidy said levelly. "I like it just fine. Keep in mind what I told you. You can leave anytime you please."

He started to say more when a hail interrupted him. It came from a good distance down the canyon, but the words carried clearly in the thin air.

"Hey, Butch," the voice called. "We've got a visitor."

Cassidy's eyes narrowed. "That's from Bill's lookout. Can't be anything threatening. He said only a visitor." He raised his voice. "Bring him in, Carver."

Kale felt his muscles loosening. It wasn't another posse looking for them. If Cassidy wasn't worried, why should he be?

Kale heard the sound of hoofs long before he saw the horses. Then the two riders came into view. He knew Carver all right, but the second rider was a complete stranger.

Anger darkened Cassidy's face, and he burst out: "It's that damned Edison. He knows better than to come in here."

At Kale's questioning look, Cassidy explained: "He's been in here before. He used to ride with us. I got tired of the trouble he was always causing and told him to get out." His mouth was a tight, grim line. Evidently, what was between him and Edison still rankled.

Cassidy started forward, muttering to himself. "Well, I can kick him out again. This time I'll make it stick."

Four men reached the two visitors first. One of them turned his head and asked, "Butch, do you remember Hamp?"

"I remember him," Cassidy said grimly. He advanced until he stood at Edison's knee. "I thought I made it plain, Hamp, but I guess you're too thick to understand. I'm through with you. Nothing you can say can change that." He was thoroughly worked up, and his words poured out. "You always were hardheaded. That hardheadedness got Kilroy killed a couple of years ago."

Edison's face was ashen, and his lips trembled. He was in mortal fear of the man who berated him, and it showed.

158

"Wait a minute, Butch," he pleaded. "I've got some news that could be important to you. Give me a chance to speak my piece. You always prided yourself on your fairness."

Cassidy stood a moment in indecision. "Get down," he finally said. "You hungry?"

Edison's relief showed in the color that flowed into his face. "I could eat some," he confessed.

Cassidy led him toward a campfire. A big pot was suspended over it, and its bubbling contents gave off a pleasant aroma.

Edison sniffed at the savory aroma. "Smells good, Butch."

Cassidy's stern expression didn't change. Nettie was stirring the pot, and Cassidy told her: "Fill up a plate for him. And give him a cup of coffee."

Nettie filled the plate with stew and carried it over to where Edison sat. Her dislike of this man showed plainly.

Edison ducked his head and fell to eating hungrily. Men crowded around where he sat, their eyes filled with curiosity.

Cassidy waited until Edison emptied the plate, then ordered: "Get on with it. Tell me what you know that's so damned important to me."

Edison leaned forward, his face intent. "I know how you feel about me, Butch. Would I be risking my life coming back here if it wasn't important?"

Cassidy's face didn't soften. "Get on with it," he said impatiently.

Edison drew a deep breath. "What would you say if I told you I know where there's a pile of gold, big enough to blind you, just waiting for the taking."

There was that magic word again, and men crowded closer.

"I'd call you a damned liar," Cassidy said flatly.

Edison shook his head. "That's because you haven't heard all the details yet. I saw that gold. I fingered some of the nuggets. Verl Wakeman brought those nuggets into South Pass City."

That aroused no spark in Cassidy's eyes, but several

159

men drew quick breaths. Kale was rigid, his breath whistling through his nostrils.

"You've heard of Verl Wakeman?" Edison asked.

"Heard of him?" Cassidy laughed harshly. "Two of his brothers are with me right now. He even rode down here with a bunch of lawmen, trying to dig us out."

"He's been bringing sacks filled with nuggets into the bank in South Pass. Don't tell me I'm crazy. I saw him carry six sacks at one time into the bank. I talked to that banker. He said that was the twelfth sack Wakeman's brought in. He had some of those nuggets in his desk. I handled them too. That banker says it's the biggest thing that's happened around South Pass in many a year. Do you believe me now?"

"No," Cassidy said emphatically. "Where was this gold supposed to come from. Gold played out in that country years ago." He looked around at the watching faces. His laugh had a nasty little ring.

"Maybe one spot was overlooked," Edison persisted. "I asked that banker where he thought that gold came from. He wouldn't tell me if he knew. But he gave me his guess. He thinks it came from Indian Charley's long-lost mine. You've heard of that?"

Cassidy impatiently shook his head. "Who hasn't, if they hung around South Pass very long? I've been hearing about it from the first day I stopped there."

"But it could happen," Edison persisted. "That banker said the Wakeman twins spent several years trying to find it. He guesses that Verl Wakeman took up the search and finally located it. Wakeman's not shipping his gold right now. He's going to let it mount up until he's cleaned out the mine. Butch, can't you see? There's a fortune waiting in that bank vault."

There was determination in Cassidy's shaking head. "I still don't believe it. I think the whole thing about Indian Charley was blown up out of a myth. Men told and retold it until they got to believing it themselves. I say it never existed from the very start."

"*I* believe it," Kale howled. His face was enflamed. "I've known about that mine ever since I was a kid. Me and Kyle"—he glanced at his brother—"hunted for that mine until we gave up. But I always believed it existed."

160

His tone grew bitter. "And that damned Verl kept hunting until he found it. Goddamn it," he said passionately. "It's not his. It belongs to Kyle and me." He took a step toward Cassidy, his expression pleading. "Don't you see, Butch? That old story has some basis to it. There's a fortune waiting for anybody with enough guts to go after it."

Cassidy was unperturbed at the implication. "Or lacks the brains to see what he could be riding into. Any of you feel the same way Kale apparently does? All you have to do is forget the security you have here and ride out where the law can get a clear sweep at you."

Those hard eyes measured each face, and slowly each man shook his head. Curry put it for all of them. "I'm not putting my neck in a loop because some old story has surfaced again."

Cassidy looked at Kale. "You see how they all feel, Kale. As I told you earlier, you're free to leave anytime you choose."

He stood and pointed at Edison. "Remember what I told you. I want you out of here first thing in the morning." He walked away without looking back.

Edison's face was bitter with frustration. Cassidy not only disbelieved him, Edison hadn't gained any favor with Cassidy for bringing this information to him.

"Wait," he begged as men started away. "It's there. I saw it."

Only Curry paused. "Hamp, I think you ought to get your head examined. A man would be a damned fool to risk his neck on such flimsy evidence as you brought." He sauntered away whistling.

Only Kale and Kyle remained near Edison. Kale's face was flushed, and his breathing was labored. "I believe you," he said passionately. "That gold's there, all right. Isn't it, Kyle?"

Kyle nodded reluctantly. "I think it's there," he said simply.

Edison seized on this last, fading hope. "Then, the three of us can go after it. I'd like to see the smugness wiped off Butch's face when he hears what he tossed away."

He looked uneasily from Kale to Kyle. "Can just the three of us handle it?"

"We can handle it," Kale said positively. "That bank is a flimsy old building, and nobody knows we're coming. We could get in, grab the gold, and be gone before anybody can think the second time."

"Then, you're going?" Edison asked eagerly.

Kale thought about Etta. How would she feel about this? He had known her so well he couldn't stand the thought of losing her.

"I'll have to talk it over with somebody," he muttered and walked away.

Etta was as evasive as she had been the last few nights. Kale had a hard time pinning her down. "Damn it, Etta," he said furiously. "Will you quit fretting and let me talk?"

His rising temper unleashed hers. "You promised me better than this," she accused him. "And what do I get? Wound up stuck in a hole like this."

"That's what I'm trying to talk about," Kale said with all the patience he could muster. "Did you see that stranger ride in this afternoon?"

She cut her eyes sideways at him. Things had gotten so bad she wouldn't look directly at Kale.

"I saw him," she said indifferently. "Nettie said he was Hamp Edison. She didn't think much of him."

"I don't give a damn what she thinks of him," Kale yelled. "Will you just listen?"

She nodded without letting him see her face. "Go ahead."

"Edison came from South Pass City. He brought along some news that will change both our lives. From now on, you won't have to worry about living in this hole. You can live anyplace you want."

"More promises?" she sniffed.

He seized her forearm, and his fingers had a bite that made her wince. "Will you shut up and just listen?" he roared.

His grip frightened her enough so that she fell silent.

Kale told her everything Edison told Cassidy. "That gold's there. I know it." His breathing eased. He had her full attention. She was listening now.

He told her of the long days he and Kyle had searched for Indian Charley's mine. "And that damned Verl winds up finding it." The bitterness crept back into his voice. "But maybe he's doing us a favor. Edison says Verl intends to leave the gold in the bank until he's ready to cash all of it in."

She was wide-eyed as she looked at him. "How much do you suppose there is, Kale?"

Kale made an impatient gesture. "I don't know. At the least, you can count on a fortune."

She was shaking with excitement now. "What do we do about it, Kale?"

"We ride back to South Pass, make a quick grab for that gold, then get away before anybody knows what's happening."

Kyle came over, and Kale said, "I've made up my mind, Kyle. We're going after that gold."

"I figured you would." Kyle didn't sound depressed or elated. He just sounded dull, as though accepting the inevitable.

"Have you thought of how you're going to get into that bank, Kale?" his brother asked.

Kale snorted. "That door is so flimsy that you can ram your shoulder against it and split it wide open."

"I'm not thinking of the door," Kyle said quietly. "I'm thinking of getting into the vault."

"I'll blow the door off of that," Kale replied. His voice quivered with eagerness. He was wrapped up in his soaring thoughts.

The shadow in Kyle's eyes brought him back to earth. "You don't like the idea," Kale snapped.

"I was thinking of the one and only time we used dynamite, Kale. That didn't turn out so well."

Kale flushed with the remembered embarrassment. "I admit I made a mistake. I won't use as much this time."

The shadow still remained in Kyle's eyes, and Kale said heatedly, "Don't you think I've learned something?"

"I hope so," Kyle said wearily.

Kale glared at him. He didn't give a damn what Kyle thought. Kale had dragged him along the way, but

163

hadn't things turned out well for them? Kale would hate to have to think about where Kyle would be right now if it wasn't for him.

"We're leaving in the morning. You, Etta, and me. Edison rides with us. I'll pick up some dynamite on the way to South Pass. Maybe I'll give Edison his share of the gold. And maybe I won't. It depends on the mood I'm in."

"Does Butch know you're leaving?"

"I'll tell him in the morning."

Kyle didn't actually shake his head, but Kale had the feeling he wanted to.

"Say what's on your mind," Kale snapped.

"Butch won't like it," Kyle murmured.

That comment stirred Kale's temper anew. At times, Kyle's stubbornness made Kale want to flatten him.

"He's already told me I could leave." He stared hard at Kyle. "Satisfied?"

Kyle fell back to the defense that had bolstered him for so many years. "Whatever you say, Kale."

The camp was just beginning to stir into life when the four rode up to Cassidy. Edison hung back, as though fear of Cassidy still held him.

"We're leaving, Butch," Kale announced.

"I thought you would," Cassidy said indifferently. "I hope to God you know what you're doing."

The old cockiness had returned to Kale. "I know." He touched the brim of his hat in a farewell salute. Cassidy was going to be a sick man when he heard how this turned out.

Chapter Twenty-eight

Verl walked over to the gun rack and took down Owen's rifle. He didn't have to tell Jabez what he was going to do. The rifle was full explanation.

"It's only been ten days," Jabez said in feeble objection. "I thought you said it'd take them twelve days if they were coming."

"That was only a rough guess, Pa," Verl said gently. "I wouldn't be very happy if they cut some time off that estimation. If they do come, I just want to be damned sure I'm there."

Jabez's expression showed that his head was filled with unsaid words. Verl hoped he didn't try to express them. He didn't want anything to weaken him now. He just wanted this over. He could guess at some of the thoughts in Jabez's mind. Verl was the only son that Jabez claimed. Jabez was living in secret dread of losing Verl.

Verl gently touched his shoulder. "Look for me when you see me coming, Pa."

He hesitated at the door. "I'll stop by and ask Carl Anderson to look in and see how you're doing."

Jabez found his tongue. "You just watch yourself, son."

"I intend to," Verl said softly. He closed the door behind him.

He saddled Jigger, thinking of the things that had to be done. He had to tell Ann and Cleatis what was happening; he had to tell John Evans the watch was on.

He knocked on the Farbers' door, and Ann let him in.

"Cleatis up yet?"

Her eyes searched his face. She saw something there that frightened her, but she wisely asked no questions.

"He's in the kitchen, Verl," she replied.

Cleatis read something in Verl's face too, for he said: "Sh! You think it's beginning."

"It could be, Cleatis," Verl corrected him. "I don't know the exact time, but I'm going to watch the bank. That's all I can promise you." As an afterthought he added, "Maybe nothing will happen."

Cleatis breathed gustily. "I hope to God everything turns out the way you want."

"Me too," Verl said gravely. God, how he wanted this over. He wanted to go back to normal living without this burden, which seemed to grow in intensity.

Ann walked with him to the front door. She kissed him before she asked, "Do you know what you're going to do?"

He regarded her fondly. What a woman. She didn't try to weaken a man with recriminations or worries. She recognized that when he had to do something she had to step back and let him do it.

"Sanderson's store is across the street from the bank. I think he'll let me watch from there." For a moment, a rush of hopelessness almost overwhelmed him. "Lord, Ann, I feel like a blind man groping his way in a world of sighted people. If I spend several days watching and nothing happens, I'll feel like a damned fool."

She patted his arm. "I have a feeling something will happen. You just be careful. I want you back."

He smiled at her. "With that in mind, how could I be careless?"

He started to move, and she said, "I'll bring some food down."

"I'd appreciate that," he said gratefully.

She frowned as a thought occurred to her. "Verl, you don't plan to be on watch twenty-four hours a day?"

At his nod, she said sternly: "What are you trying to do? Kill yourself?"

He grinned lightheartedly. "Hadn't really planned on that, Ann." That didn't erase her frown, and he said quietly: "I can't pull anybody else into this, Ann. I

166

can't risk getting them hurt. It's not their affair. Don't you see?" he asked, trying to coax a smile back into her face.

She showed her first weakness, for she wailed, "Oh God, I wish it was over."

"Both of us, Ann," he said soberly.

He looked back after he mounted. She still stood in the door. He touched his hat, then turned Jigger. A bad time, he thought unhappily as he rode toward the bank. A time of strain without having an inkling of how it will end, or when.

He tied Jigger to the hitch rack and walked inside. "John in?"

Ed Dehner nodded. "I think he's sort of expecting you. He's been on edge the last couple of days."

Verl stepped into the office, and Evans was pacing the floor. He stopped abruptly, as though he had been caught doing something shameful. "I thought you guessed Kale and Kyle would be back here in about twelve days."

"I did," Verl admitted. "But I got to fretting, like you're doing." He grinned at the flush in Evans' face. "It won't hurt any to be here a little early. I just wanted to tell you I'll be in Sanderson's store, if you want me for any reason."

"You're not taking this on alone, are you, Verl?"

"I have to," Verl said simply "Hell, John, I've done a lot of thinking about it. I couldn't go to the law and tell what I have in mind. If they didn't think I was crazy, they'd laugh me out of the office. Can't see any other way," he finished simply.

Evans sighed and shook his head. "Guess not, Verl. You watch your step."

"I intend to," Verl answered and walked out of the office. Three different people had warned him to be careful. If good wishes meant anything, he was well wrapped in them.

He walked into Sanderson's store, and Ross Sanderson asked, "What can I do for you, Verl?"

"A big favor, Ross. I've got a hunch Kale and Kyle will be coming back. I think they intend to rob the bank." He looked across the street. Sanderson's front window gave him an excellent view of the bank building and the front door. He didn't have to worry about a back door. The bank didn't have one.

He grinned at the alarmed flash in Sanderson's eyes. "That's where the favor comes in. I want to watch the bank door from your store. I'm hoping to stop the robbery before it even gets a chance to start."

"I'm with you in that, Verl." Sanderson's uneasiness didn't completely vanish. Verl could appreciate that. This was the first time Sanderson had been involved in any possible violence, and he couldn't help but be nervous. "Are you in this alone?" Sanderson asked. At Verl's nod he exploded. "That's damned foolish, Verl. You should call on the law for some help."

Verl grinned wryly. "That's the big trouble, Ross. I don't know when it might happen, if it happens at all. It might be tonight, tomorrow, or any day you might pick for the next couple of weeks. You can imagine how the law would react if I told them something like this."

He chuckled at Sanderson's perplexity. "I'm not even sure they're coming. I just think they might."

"You never forgot about Owen," Sanderson almost whispered.

"I haven't." Verl's words were crisp. "I won't rest easy, and I don't think Owen will, until those two are stopped." His eyes were unseeing at the moment. "The family should have seen Kale and Kyle turning bad a long time ago. But we made excuses for them because they were family. It's time I made up for those excuses.

"Don't look so mournful, Ross. I came in to ask if I can watch from your store."

"You know you can," Sanderson responded promptly. He moved to the back of the store and returned, carrying an old rocking chair.

"I've rocked many an hour in it. I hope you find it as comforting as I have."

"It'll do just fine," Verl said heartily.

Verl took the chair from Sanderson. He chose a spot just to one side of the window. By craning his neck a little, he could still get a view of the bank's front door.

He wouldn't be too obvious to anybody passing down the street.

"This in your way?" Verl asked.

"Not at all," Sanderson said stoutly.

"Good. Go on about your business as normally as you can," Verl said. "Oh, Ross," he called Sanderson back. "If anybody makes any comment about my being here, you don't know anything about it. As far as you know, I'm just loafing."

Sanderson stared reproachfully at him. "You know I won't talk, Verl."

"Sure, I do," Verl said and grinned. "But some of these nosy women can dig pretty hard. I just don't want you saying anything to anybody."

Sanderson shook his head as a further reproach and hurried to meet a woman just coming in the door.

The woman was a prospective customer, and Verl heard her chattering away. She talked of petty, inconsequential things, and Sanderson answered her absently. Sanderson's thoughts were occupied by the man in the rocking chair.

Verl learned what people meant when they talked about the slow passage of time. The afternoon hours wore away, and Verl's butt grew numb. He stood several times and stamped a few circles around the chair. This waiting was going to be the hardest part.

He glanced at the Seth Thomas clock on the wall. He was surprised that it was a little after six o'clock. No matter how wearing time was, it eventually passed.

Sanderson's store was empty, and Verl thought sure Sanderson would be locking up. Business hadn't been brisk—it rarely was on a weekday—and Verl expected Sanderson to take advantage of the lack of business to close early.

He waited until Sanderson came over to him, then asked, "Aren't you about ready to go home?"

"Not this time," Sanderson said firmly.

Verl's eyebrows raised, and he said crossly: "If you got any fool idea in your head, forget it. I told you I could handle it alone. If you don't mind, I'll stay here all night."

"Yes, and be dead in the morning," Sanderson retorted. "Verl, don't argue with me. I'm not going to get into this." A little shiver passed through him. 'Lord, I wouldn't know what to do. But I can help you in one way. While you grab a few winks, I can watch the bank for you. I know Kale and Kyle. I'll awaken you if they appear."

Verl was touched by the offer. To cover his feelings, he said roughly: "How about *your* sleep? You've got a business to run tomorrow."

"When you're awake, I can doze," Sanderson said cheerfully. "Never was much of a sleeper anyway."

This was the part Verl had worried about. He intended to go this alone, but he didn't know how long he would last, particularly if the waiting period dragged out. He would be so worn out it would be hard to keep his eyes open. Thanks to Sanderson, that abrasive period was all smoothed out.

"I'm grateful to you," Verl said huskily.

"Forget it," Sanderson said abruptly. "Be right back."

Verl watched him curiously. Sanderson moved along the shelves stocked with canned goods. Every now and then, Sanderson reached up and selected a can. He came back carrying canned beef, tomatoes, and peaches. He even stopped at a barrel to fill a brown paper bag with crackers.

"Not the fanciest meal in the world," he said cheerfully. "But you won't starve."

"You didn't have to do this," Verl protested.

"Not doing it for you. I'm hungry too."

"Then you're going to put it on the Wakeman bill."

"The hell I will. Can't a man have a guest in now and then?" He pulled a can opener from his pocket. "Work on these cans while I go get another chair."

Verl had the cans opened when Sanderson returned. Sanderson set his chair beside Verl's, and they ate, passing the cans back and forth.

"I'm telling you the truth," Verl said sincerely. "Best food I ever tasted. This is a banquet."

170

Sanderson chuckled. "I never went to any special pains."

Verl laughed, the first time in a long while he had felt so inclined.

"Gets dark early," Verl commented as he watched the shadows thicken along the street.

"Expect them after dark, Verl?"

"I don't know when to expect them," Verl said honestly. He peered across the street. There was no moon, but he could still make out the bank door.

"Ah," he murmured with satisfaction. "I can see anybody who might fool around with that door."

Sanderson looked across the street. "I see that door too," he said, and his relief showed. "I wasn't too sure of my eyes, but now I know I can be of some use to you. You take a snooze while I watch." He guessed at the hesitation in Verl and said impatiently, "Oh, hell. I won't do anything on my own. I'm not *that* crazy. If I see anybody over there, I'll just wake you up."

Verl was satisfied he could depend on Sanderson, but he didn't think he was sleepy yet. "I'll just close my eyes, Ross."

He was pretty certain he wouldn't drift off, but the long strain was demanding its toll.

He came awake with a start, and for a moment didn't know where he was. He stared wildly about, and it came slowly back to him. He looked out at the street, and it was bathed in moonlight. He knew the moon didn't come up until midnight, and he looked accusingly at Sanderson. "You let me sleep."

Sanderson chuckled. "What was wrong with that? Nothing was happening. You looked so peaceful."

Verl stood to stretch the kinks out of his muscles. He rolled his shoulders again. "I'm grateful, Ross. I'm good for the rest of the night. You go ahead and sleep. Better yet, why don't you go home?"

Sanderson shook his head stubbornly. "No, I'd like to see how this winds up. But I'll go back to the storeroom. I've got a pallet there. Lord, if I slept in this chair like you did, I wouldn't be able to move."

171

He stopped before he moved off. "You really think they'll come?"

"Yes," Verl said, a determined ring in his voice. "I'm just a little early. I figured on that."

Sanderson sighed at the expanse of waiting time that could be ahead. "It would be nice if you could pinpoint it."

Verl chuckled. "It sure would. Then I could go rent a hotel room and leave a call for a certain time. I've got a hunch Kale will pick one of two times: early in the morning, or after dark. I don't think even he would pick a time when the street is busy."

Sanderson's hand rested briefly on Verl's shoulder before he ambled off toward the rear of the room.

Damned good man wrapped up in that mild, inoffensive exterior, Verl thought as he watched him go.

He went back to watching the bank, trying to keep his mind a blank. The less he thought about what drove him, the better he could endure it.

Verl was never so glad to see the sun come up, ending the long, unproductive night. Damn but he was stiff, and it took several minutes to work it out. What he needed was an active job to do. He would like nothing better than to have an ax in his hands, standing before a huge pile of wood that needed cutting up.

Sanderson looked seedy when he came out of the rear room. "I didn't intend to sleep that long," he grumbled.

"I'm glad you did," Verl said, and meant it.

Sanderson ran the back of his finger across his chin. "I need a shave."

Verl nodded. He did too. "And I'd like a bath thrown in. Ross, you can't keep this up. I told you before, it's not your job."

Verl thought uneasiness flickered in Sanderson's eyes, but Sanderson said stoutly enough, "We'll see how another night goes."

Verl knew him well enough not to try to turn him.

Ann came into the store an hour later, carrying a basket covered with a towel.

She looked at Verl and asked, "Bad night, Verl?"

"No, quiet. What makes you ask that?"

"The way you look." She smiled at him. "You look rough."

"I feel it too," he confessed.

She handed him the basket. "Maybe this will make you feel better."

He uncovered the basket, and warmth filled his eyes at the sight of the fried chicken there. "You're something, Ann," he said.

Color touched her face. "There's some potato salad there too. I couldn't think of any way of keeping the chicken warm. I'll bet you didn't eat anything last night."

"Then you'd lose," he retorted. "Ross fed me. We ate out of cans."

"That's awful, Verl."

He shook his head. "Not as bad as that. I kind of enjoyed it. Not as much as I'll enjoy this. Can I share this with Ross?"

Smilingly, she nodded.

Sanderson came over at Verl's call.

"Ross, look what Ann brought us."

Sanderson beamed as he took his first bite. "Disappointed in you, Ann. This is merely wonderful. I expected you to do better."

"I'll try to remember that," Ann said serenely. Her eyes were radiant, her cheeks flushed. She was a supremely happy woman.

The happiness didn't last too long, for stern reality caught her up again.

"Verl, what do you think now?"

"I told you I was going into this blind," he said frankly. "Nothing's cleared up. But I picked tomorrow as the day they would make a try, if they intended to. I've got a queer hunch it could happen. All I can do is wait and see."

She briefly closed her eyes, and Verl knew she was going through some kind of torment, but she didn't speak of it.

She looked at him and managed a wan smile. "I'd better be getting back." She gathered up her towel and basket and stood. "I could leave the bones, Verl. You might get hungry."

He grinned. "As good as that chicken was, I'd be tempted to try the bones." '

"He won't get hungry," Sanderson promised. "It won't be as good as what you brought, but he'll get by."

Ann pressed Sanderson's hand. "I'm grateful for what you've done for him, Ross."

That got to Sanderson, for it showed in the warmth stealing into his cheeks. "It wasn't much."

"It was everything," she corrected. "I don't know how he could've gotten through without you."

She looked longingly at Verl, and he wondered if the same impulse was in her mind. He'd give anything to kiss her.

She shook herself and said briskly: "I'll be back in the morning. Maybe it'll be a better day."

"We'll hope for that," Verl said gravely. He watched Ann leave the store.

"Fine woman," Sanderson observed.

"None better," Verl agreed.

Sanderson sighed. "Another day, Verl. I hope it passes quicker than last night."

Verl chuckled wryly. "We're thinking along the same line, Ross."

"Maybe this will be a light day," Sanderson said hopefully. "Right now, I'd be just as happy if not a single customer came in."

Verl settled himself into the chair. Lord, he was going to detest this thing before it was over. A rocking chair might comfort a man for a short period, but in the long run it could kill him.

The day passed uneventfully, and Sanderson opened some more cans after the store closed. "Not as good as Ann's chicken," he said disparagingly.

Verl grinned. "Who's complaining?"

He insisted that Sanderson sleep the first hours of the night. "Take as long as you need, Ross. I'm not a bit sleepy." That wasn't just talk. Oddly enough, he felt keyed up.

It was well after midnight when Sanderson appeared

again. "Get some sleep, Verl. I'll awaken you if I see anything."

Verl yawned. "I can go to sleep now. Lord, Ross, I'll never get out of your debt."

That tickled Sanderson. "Then, I'll hold it over your head the rest of your life."

As keyed up as Verl was, he thought it might be difficult to fall asleep. He was wrong. He closed his eyes and didn't remember anything after that.

A soft, insistent hand shook him awake. Verl fought returning to awareness. He had been sleeping so well.

"Verl," a voice whispered in his ear. "Three men just coming down the street toward the bank. It's after dawn, but I can't make them out for sure yet."

Chapter Twenty-nine

Four horses pulled up at the outskirts of South Pass City. Kale looked at Etta. She looked tired, but her eyes sparkled. The anticipation of what was ahead far overcame the weariness of the long ride.

"Told you we'd make it on the sixth day," Kale crowed. "We'll hit the bank just when I want. Right after dawn."

Kyle was in a grumpy mood. "It took half the night of hard riding to do it," he said sourly. "I don't see what difference another day would have made."

Kyle's ill humor wasn't going to dampen Kale's spirits. "The sooner we get our hands on that gold, the happier I'll be. Right, Hamp?"

"You said it, Kale," Edison replied. He hoped the spreading tightness inside him would lessen. The sooner this was over, the better it would suit him.

"Etta," Kale said, "we'll ride on into town. Nobody

will be up at this hour. I'll leave the horses with you right around the corner from the bank. I'll probably have to use dynamite to get the vault open. When you hear that blast, you bring the horses to the bank as fast as you can." His eyes were hard and shining. "Do you understand everything? A lot depends on you."

She was so eager she was trembling. "I won't let you down, Kale."

"That's the way I'm figuring," he said. He pulled an extra pistol from his waistband and handed it to her. "You know how to use it. Don't hesitate if anything goes wrong."

"I promise," she said, her mouth a thin, determined line.

Verl focused his eyes on the three figures slinking along in front of the bank. In a few more strides they would be at the bank door. Sanderson might not be sure who those men were, but Verl knew them. Kale and Kyle had returned, and they had brought Edison with them.

It had gone just as Verl figured. He didn't think Cassidy would fall for that trumped-up story about a gold find, but Edison was a different matter. That made three to contend with instead of two. At this stage it didn't matter.

Verl reached down beside the chair and picked up Owen's rifle. "It's *them*, Ross. Time to go."

Sanderson was literally wringing his hands in distress. "I wish I could help you, Verl. But I'd be helpless out there."

Verl touched him on the shoulder. "You've already done more than enough." He walked to the door, opened it, and stepped outdoors.

The three had reached the bank door and were working at it, their backs toward Verl. Verl thought he saw the flash of light from something long and metallic. Probably a pinch bar, he thought.

It was odd how calm he felt. His thoughts were sharp and lucid. He reasoned that the long wait was over, and the strain was gone.

176

"That's enough, Kale," he called. "Turn around real slow. There's nothing inside that bank." That might be childish, but he wanted Kale to know he had been duped. His rifle was at his hip, the muzzle aimed at Kale. Those were his brothers over there, but that old relationship had no claim on him. He would shoot at the first sign of resistance. If they wanted to surrender, he might accept that and turn them over to the law. He felt a weary resignation. He guessed that the old relationship did have a small hold on him.

The three figures straightened, and Verl thought every muscle in them went rigid. They were as motionless as carved statues, and Verl knew what a shock this was to all of them.

"I said turn around," he snapped. "Make it slow and easy."

He couldn't have waited more than a few seconds before they started turning, but it seemed like an eon.

There was nothing slow and easy about their turn. Kale whirled before the others did. His face was a contorted mask, and his voice was harsh and filled with rage.

"Goddamn you, Verl," he screamed. The realization of what Verl had done was in those words. "I'll kill you for tricking me."

He wanted to, and God knew he tried. His hand dipped toward the butt of the holstered gun, but he never reached it.

Verl shot him as dispassionately as though he was shooting at some inanimate target.

"Damn you," Kyle yelled. "You killed Kale."

"Yes," Verl said coldly. "Give it up, Kyle. You followed him for too long."

Kyle was beyond the reach of sanity. He grabbed for his gun, and Verl was ready for that too. He pulled the trigger again, and Kyle's face went taut with shock. He stared at Verl, then pitched forward on his face to lie in the street with Kale.

Edison's eyes were literally bulging. It had all happened too fast for him to comprehend.

Verl swung the rifle to cover Edison. "You can join them," he invited coldly.

Edison looked at that cold, savage face, then slowly his hands went into the air. "Not me," he begged. "I don't want any part of your family fight."

It was over, but Verl felt no elation. He only felt infinitely weary. They were still his brothers, and he couldn't get that out of his mind.

"Unbuckle your gun belt, Edison," he said, and moved to the middle of the street.

"What are you going to do with me?" Edison asked sullenly as his fingers fumbled at the buckle.

Verl waited until the gun belt plopped onto the wooden walk. "Turn you over to the law," he said in a remote voice. "I imagine the law will find enough charges to hold you for a long time."

He heard the sudden hard beat of hoofs, and whipped his head about. He got a blurred impression of a rider coming at him pell-mell. He wasn't sure who the rider was, but he had the feeling it was small and feminine.

"You killed Kale," a voice screamed at him. "Damn you." Sobs almost broke up the words. "You killed Kale."

Verl realized it was Etta rushing straight at him. He would have tried to reason with her, but there wasn't time. The horse was almost upon him.

He still might have hesitated, but she was shooting at him. The first bullet plowed into the dirt between his feet, and the second one slammed into his left side just below the shoulder.

The impact of the bullet knocked him backward, and he dropped the rifle. He tried to retain his balance, but it was a losing battle. He hit the ground hard, his eyes blurring and a sickness filling his stomach.

Etta raced by him, whirled the horse, and came back again.

Verl's hand shook as he fumbled for his pistol. He got a hazy glimpse of her face. It was tear-stained and furious.

Nothing was going to stop her. She was either going

to trample him under her horse's hoofs, or she was going to shoot him again. He was vaguely aware that two more angry slugs gouged the dust beside him.

"Etta," he yelled feebly. "Use your head. I don't want to—"

He didn't finish, for she was whirling her horse again, and she was coming back. He thought his words were loud and ringing, but they were only a whisper. He realized she hadn't heard him at all. Even if she had, he doubted words alone could stop her. She had only one thought in that enraged mind: to kill.

Verl tried to aim the pistol, but it was an uncoordinated effort. His eyes were getting more blurred, and he cursed them mentally. How could he stop her if he couldn't see her?

He pulled the trigger, and a blackness descended upon him like a thick cloud that encompassed everything. He thought he heard a shrill, agonized scream that didn't sound quite human.

It was pure relief to let go and fall into that deep, black hole that waited for him. He didn't see the horse fall.

He lay there, listening to the babble of voices, trying to figure where they all came from. A moment ago, there hadn't been anybody in the street. How had all these people been drawn so quickly? He tried to sort out the annoying questions. He just wished, wearily, that all the voices would go away. They kept prodding at him, urging him to open his eyes, and he didn't want to. It was much more comfortable in this darkened world he was in.

"Verl, Verl," a soft voice kept insisting. "Can you hear me?

That voice had a familiar ring, and that was another puzzle to solve. Who was it? Then it came to him in a rush. It was Ann. He didn't know how she had gotten here so fast, but she was here. Hell, yes, he wanted to talk to her.

He kept fighting those heavy eyelids until he forced them open.

"He's coming to," a voice said. It, too, had a familiar ring, but at the moment, it was another voice he couldn't place. His eyes weren't working well at all. All he could see of Ann was a blurred outline of her face. She might be crying, but he wasn't sure. Damn, but he hurt. He tried to smile, but didn't know it was only a grimace.

"Hello, Ann," he said weakly. He didn't want her to see him lying in the street, and he started to get up. Just raising his shoulders sent a piercing stab of pain all through his left side.

Ann placed a hand on his shoulder to hold him in place. "Don't you try anything so foolish again," she stormed.

Verl looked curiously at her. Her face was white and drawn, but her eyes were flashing. She meant what she said. But why should she be so angry with him?

"You've been badly wounded," she said. "The doctor just finished patching you up. Do you want to tear that wound open?"

Verl rested, waiting for the bolts of pain to lessen. He looked about him. He wasn't in the street at all; he was lying on the floor of Sanderson's store. He could pick out Sanderson's anxious face, and he wanted to wink and tell him that everything was just fine, but he wasn't up to the effort of trying to lie.

"How did I get in here?" he asked. Things were beginning to return to him. The last he remembered he had been in the street, and Etta had been doing her utmost to kill him.

"People carried you in, Verl. Somebody ran and got the doctor. You've been unconscious for three hours. You don't remember any of that?"

Verl shook his head. He had to tell Ann something, and he dreaded that. But perhaps she already knew. But if that was true, why did she seem concerned only about him? He knew Etta's horse had fallen. He had just killed her sister. That alone would put a wide chasm between them.

"Ann," he said haltingly. "I'm sorry about Etta."

"I'm sorry too," she said briskly. "But she asked for what she got."

180

He stared at her, bewildered. He never would have thought Ann would be so callous. What she said about Etta earning what she got was true, but he would have expected her to show some grief over the death of her sister.

"I didn't want to kill her. But she kept coming at me, shooting all the time. I couldn't stop her any other way."

"She sure did," Sanderson broke in excitedly. "I stood in the window and saw it all. I guess your shots at Kale and Kyle drew her, for she came tearing down the street like a bat out of hell. I thought sure she was going to get you."

"I guess losing Kale drove her crazy," Verl muttered. "I didn't want to shoot her, Ann." He felt no regret over Kale and Kyle, but Etta was a woman.

"You didn't shoot Etta," Ann said softly. "You hit her horse. It fell on her. Her back was broken. The doctor says that she may never walk again." Her eyes were far away, as though she were looking at some distant scene. "Poor Etta," she murmured. "She always sought excitement, even when she was small." Ann's eyes misted with tears. "What happened to her will hold her as well as a jail cell. Unless the law wants to punish her further." Now there was real anxiety in her voice.

Verl managed to shake his head. "I don't think they will, Ann." He felt a tremendous relief at the way this turned out. Cleatis might not be too happy, but he had his daughter back.

He turned his head at the sound of wheels in the street. They sounded as though they were stopping. "Who's that?" he asked in mild curiosity.

Ann stood and looked out into the street. "Somebody went after Jabez. Tom Anderson brought him in."

Verl winced. He didn't know how this would hit Jabez, but it had to be hard. He had lost two more sons.

Jabez limped in, Tom Anderson and Dr. Harley after him.

Harley pushed his way ahead of the other two and looked down at Verl. "Ah, so you came to," he murmured. "For a moment, you had me concerned."

"We all were, Doctor," Ann said softly.

181

Harley knelt down and examined the wound in Verl's side. "Well, it hasn't broken open," he said with satisfaction. "Considering how much blood you lost, your color's surprisingly good. I think you're going to make it." His face turned severe. "But you're going to take it easy, until that wound is thoroughly healed. Do you understand me?"

Verl nodded meekly. "Doc, how is Etta?"

"Doing as well as can be expected," Harley said brusquely. "She'll never forget this morning."

A hand pulled at Harley's shoulder, and Harley turned his head and frowned. "All right, Jabez. You can talk to him now. But only for a few minutes. I don't want him disturbed too much."

Jabez grunted as he kneeled down beside Verl. "How you doing, son?" he asked gruffly.

"Real good, Pa." It had to be said now, and he hesitated, choosing the right words. There was no easy way to say this. "It's all over. I killed Kale and Kyle."

For a moment, Jabez's face twisted. "It had to be done," he said flatly. "Did Kale and Kyle come alone?"

Verl hadn't thought about Edison until now. He looked questioningly at Sanderson, and Sanderson grinned in delight.

"He tore out, Verl," Sanderson said. "Like the devil was after him."

Jabez shrugged. "It doesn't matter. We didn't want him. Now we can forget all about it. You're coming home with me, Verl, where I can take care of you."

"No, he isn't," Harley said. "That ride to your place wouldn't be the best thing for him now. Two or three weeks, and he should be able to return home."

Jabez's face darkened. "But where will he stay? I can't just go away and leave him here alone."

"He won't be alone," Ann said serenely. "He can mend at our house. I think that will suit the doctor?" She glanced questioningly at Harley.

Harley nodded. "That will do just fine." He glanced speculatively at Ann, then at Verl. "A woman's care is just what he needs."

Jabez's face still showed concern. He wasn't ready to quit arguing.

182

Verl closed his eyes in contentment. Let Ann and Jabez argue it out, but Verl knew who would win. He didn't have to worry about Jabez. The Andersons would see that he was all right until Verl got well.

He listened to the sound of Ann's and Jabez's voices, at times showing a little heat. You might as well give up, Pa, he thought. You're up against something stronger than you ever knew. You're up against a woman's will. He knew where he was going to wind up. At Ann's house. Nothing could have pleased him more.